Summer had some other peculiarities too, like rocking her body when she was upset, just rocking and moaning. Or shaking her leg. That would drive her teachers nuts, and they would always put her in the back row, so they wouldn't see that leg going to town.

And Summer talked to herself. People would laugh at her when they caught her doing it, especially the other kids. And she would turn real red in the face. She told me secretly that beings appeared to her that nobody else could see, and that's who she was talking to.

I got mad at folks when they laughed at Summer, but as she got older she started whispering to the invisible ones, instead of talking out loud, so others were not as apt to notice. She was always looking up toward the hills, listening and whispering. And I didn't think Summer strange at all, because she was my sister and I had grown up with her whispering to the hills.

RUTH WHITE is the author of *Sweet Creek Holler,* *Weeping Willow,* and *Belle Prater's Boy,* which was a Newbery Honor Book and is available in a Dell Yearling edition. She lives in Pennsylvania.

Memories of Summer

Ruth White

Published by
Dell Laurel-Leaf
an imprint of
Random House Children's Books
a division of Random House, Inc.
1540 Broadway
New York, New York 10036

Visit us on the Web! www.randomhouse.com/teens

Educators and librarians, for a variety of teaching tools, visit us at www.randomhouse.com/teachers

ISBN: 0-440-22921-9

RL: 5.0

Reprinted by arrangement with Farrar Straus Giroux

Printed in the United States of America

May 2002

10 9 8 7 6 5 4 3 2

If someone loves a flower, of which just one single
blossom grows in all the millions and millions of stars,
it is enough to make him happy just to look at the stars.
He can say to himself,
"Somewhere, my little flower is there . . ."

—*The Little Prince* by Antoine de Saint-Exupéry

MEMORIES OF SUMMER

one

My parents knew no other place but the southwest Virginia hills where they were raised. I didn't remember Mama, because she died of consumption when I was three and my sister was six. But relatives told us she had been a gentle person who read poetry and the Bible, and sang hymns beautifully.

We affectionately called our daddy Poppy, and many times he related to us what Mama had decided long before we were born.

"Our children will have no common names," she had said to him. "A name should have meaning, and tell other folks something about the person. It should help you find your place in this life, and make you feel like you're worth something."

So when my older sister was born, Mama had said, "We'll call this one Summer, and she'll grow up just a'sparklin' with warmth and laughter, and the world will be a brighter place with her in it."

And when I was born, Mama had said, "We'll call this

one Lyric, and she'll be a singer of songs so sweet it'll bring tears to your eyes."

Poppy spent a year watching Mama waste away to nothing before she finally died, and he always said it was the sorriest year of his life, not just because he lost her, but on top of that, his daddy, our Grandpa Compton, died in a mining accident. Poppy told us he hoped and prayed his girls would never have to suffer through a time like that.

Everybody in Glory Bottom knew Grandpa. When the explosion boomed, Grandpa and six other men were trapped in this little bitty space, cut off from the rest of the mine, sealed in tight as a tomb. The foreman, who had been away to the college and knew about such things, calculated how long they could survive in this small area cramped with seven bodies breathing. And what he said was if they were still and didn't exert too much energy, and didn't breathe any more than was necessary, they had maybe an hour to live. So they sat quiet and waited and prayed for deliverance before the hour was up.

Grandpa was the only one wearing a watch, and ever so often he would hold it up to the carbide lamp on his miner's helmet and softly call out the time to the trapped men. The others thought it was peculiar for him to do such a thing, but they didn't mention it, maybe 'cause they were curious to know how much time they had left on this earth. But the most peculiar thing of all was when the rescuers finally got there, Grandpa was the only dead man amongst them. Somebody figured out they had been trapped almost two hours instead of one. Grandpa had called out the wrong time, making the men think they had more time than they did, just so they wouldn't give up hope. But he was wearing the watch, so only he knew the truth!

Poppy had always been a good ole boy, just happy to be a coal miner like his daddy and his daddy's daddy. But he changed after Mama and Grandpa died. Where he usta go out gambling and carousing, and spending his money on liquor, now he stayed home, and took up reading the Bible and going to church with us.

Poppy also had the reputation of being the best guitar picker this side of Nashville. He could play any tune you could hum, and he was always saying that it was his mission in life to give joy, to make people sing and dance and laugh.

So it was just as Mama had predicted—in spite of our loss of her, me and Summer grew up singing and laughing. Poppy was always there like a rock, and we felt safe and loved. Our childhood was happy.

But it was Summer I remember bathing me and kissing away the bumps and bruises. Summer patty-caking and rockabye-babying. Reading to me. Summer packing my lunch and taking me to my first day of school. Leading me by the hand to the outhouse in the morning dew. Holding my forehead when I threw up. Plaiting my hair. Hushing me in Sunday School.

We roamed the hills and creeks, picking daisies and tiger lilies, black-eyed Susans, Indian paintbrushes, and wild pink roses. We slid downhill on golden leaves. We climbed trees and explored caves, and peeped into abandoned mines. But we didn't go in there. They were scary. We dammed up the creek and made swimmin' holes. But best of all, we told each other our secrets and dreams.

Poppy had never owned a car. He didn't even know how to drive, so we walked everywhere we went. If it was too far to walk, there was a bus that went to some places. If we couldn't get there by bus, we had to find somebody with a car to take us. If we couldn't do that, we stayed home. And that's what we did most of the time. Stayed home.

We liked each other and we entertained each other. We read books and played games. We listened to the radio. We made fudge and went to quiltings, to school and church and to the picture show at the county seat. We saw relatives at Thanksgiving and Decoration Day.

Me and Summer learned to cook pretty good. Poppy helped us raise a garden, and we canned things for cold weather. We bought our clothes cheap at the company store or from a mail-order catalog. So we had everything we needed. Then why did we dream about going somewheres else and making more money and having more stuff? It's a mystery. I don't know why, but it was a continuing thread that pulled the years together. Someday we will leave this place. Someday we will have a white house. Someday we will have more money and buy things.

Poppy taught me and Summer to harmonize, and we got real good at it. Everybody said so. Summer's voice was high and clear like a bell, while mine was low and mellow like a clarinet. And people were always asking us to sing for them. We could be going down the road to the store, or coming home from the show, and somebody was liable to step out on their porch and holler, "Come on in here, girls, and sing us a song!" So we did. And they paid us nickels and dimes, sometimes quarters, depending on who it was.

We sang for fun even when we didn't get paid, simply because we loved it. Lots of times we sung places with Poppy—parties and church gatherings mostly. But any place there was an audience, they might ask us to pick and sing. I reckon we were famous in our neck of the woods.

Summer always did have funny ways about her, but I got so used to them, they seemed normal to me. For example, she was scared to death of electricity. Poppy called it a "terror" and he said it started when Summer was a baby and stuck her finger in a live socket. But Summer said she didn't even remember that, and she thought it started when she stepped on an electric cord that was frayed. Both times she was shocked.

But whenever it happened, her fear of electricity kept her from doing some ordinary things. Like pulling the cord to turn on the light in a dark room. Me or Poppy had to do that for her. She wouldn't even turn on the radio. We had to do that for her too, and then adjust the static out of it. We also had a fan that she wouldn't touch. In fact, she would pull her dress tail aside to keep from brushing it when she passed by. But the Frigidaire was something else. She wasn't a bit afraid of it. She said it was because it was cold. So it didn't seem to be electric. She thought of electricity as hot. We had nothing else that was electric, except lights on our Christmas tree once a year.

Another odd thing was Summer's fear of dogs. She would panic and hide whenever she saw one. She always called them wolves. She'd say she heard a wolf barking, or a wolf wanted to bite her, when it was really just a little doggie trying to play.

I liked dogs myself, and one time Poppy got us a puppy, hoping Summer would get over her terror. But she wouldn't have it in the house. She cried and cried until Poppy gave the puppy away to kinfolks. I didn't fault her for that. She couldn't help how she felt.

She had some other peculiarities too, like rocking her body when she was upset, just rocking and moaning. Or shaking her leg. That would drive her teachers nuts, and they would always put her in the back row, so they wouldn't see that leg going to town.

And Summer talked to herself. People would laugh at her when they caught her doing it, especially the other kids. And she would turn real red in the face. She told me secretly that beings appeared to her that nobody else could see, and that's who she was talking to.

I got mad at folks when they laughed at Summer, but as she got older she started whispering to the invisible ones, instead of talking out loud, so others were not as apt to notice. She was always looking up toward the hills, listening and whispering. And I didn't think Summer strange at all, because she was my sister and I had grown up with her whispering to the hills.

two

August 9, 1955, Summer's sixteenth birthday, was a hot day, relieved by a gentle afternoon shower, so that the deep holler where we lived between the mountains lay cool in shadows. It smelled of rain and earth.

We were on the front porch. Summer's friends Jewel and Ethel were there, as well as Anderson Biddle. He was a town boy, and that's why we called him by his whole and complete name. You did that with town folks.

I remember the sky was pink late that evening and Jewel said it meant that somebody was going to die.

" 'Course somebody's gonna die," Summer said. "Somebody dies every day!"

I had turned thirteen in March, and I could bake cakes pretty good. I baked one for Summer, and it was white with sixteen yellow candles on it. I remember how Summer's blue eyes sparkled. She looked so pretty that day.

"I wish . . . I wish . . . I wish for a black horse and a silver saddle!" she said with a giggle, and blew out the candles quick.

"Now it won't come true!" I protested. "You told!"

She slipped a butcher knife into the cake with a soft ker-plump! And when she pulled it out, there was icing curled around the sharp edges.

"It won't come true anyways," she said. "That's why I always wish for something I don't really want. Then I won't be disappointed, see?"

We had been dancing to the radio throughout the evening, and me and Summer put our arms around each other and harmonized on a song just the way Rosemary Clooney and Vera Ellen did it in a movie called *White Christmas*.

> *Sisters, sisters,*
> *There were never such devoted sisters . . .*

We had to sit through that movie four times before we got all the words right.

> *All kinds of weather, we stick together,*
> *The same in the rain and sun.*
> *Two diff'rent faces, but in tight places*
> *We think and we act as one.*
> *Uh-huh!*

That last part was especially true. One time me and Summer even dreamed the same dream. We both woke up the next morning babbling about wearing a red dress, and flying over the river. Another thing we did ever once in a while was to bust out singing the same song at the same time! It was uncanny.

There were more words to "Sisters," and we sang it all.

Our audience laughed and clapped. Summer finished cutting the cake and everybody reached for a piece. Poppy came out and sat in a rocking chair, slightly apart from us, smoking his pipe. I handed him some cake on a saucer.

We had Kool-Aid in jelly glasses, and Anderson Biddle said, "Whoo . . . ee!" as he sipped some with his face all screwed up. "It's sour enough to make a pig squeal!"

He was right. It *was* a bit short on the sugar.

"Here's my present, Summer," I said as I placed it, wrapped in soft white tissue paper, on the table that held the cake and stuff.

"Lyric! You shouldn't a'done that!" she said, but I could tell she was pleased.

It was only Precious Pink nail polish. But Summer acted like it was the crown jewels. She always tried to make me feel good like that.

Anderson Biddle gave her a great big bottle of Evening in Paris, and Ethel and Jewel, her *so-called* friends, didn't give her anything. When we were quiet again, everybody looked toward Poppy. We were wondering what he had got for his oldest girl on her sixteenth birthday. For a few days now he had been acting like the cat that swallowed the canary.

"I don't have a proper wrapped-up gift, Summer," he said. "Just some good news."

Summer pushed brown hair out of her pretty face with sticky fingers and looked at him.

"But it's my gift to you," Poppy went on, trying not to smile. "I saved it 'specially for your birthday."

"News 'bout what?"

We looked at Poppy, quiet and waiting.

For a moment even the frogs and crickets quit their evening chatter, and listened for the thing Poppy had to say. Jewel and Ethel and Anderson Biddle stopped eating.

"We're finally moving to Michigan."

"No foolin'?" Summer said breathlessly.

"You got the money?" I said.

"Yeah, I managed to squeeze out the last few dollars we need for bus fare. And Henry wrote me last week. He's found us a place to live. It's even got furniture in it."

Now he was smiling outright.

"All the way to Michigan?" I said in a whisper.

"What's in Michigan?" Anderson Biddle said.

Hadn't he heard all the talk about the car industry in Michigan, how it was booming up there, and anybody could get a job? I guess not.

"We're going to Flint, where they make Chevrolets and Buicks," Summer said. "Poppy's friend Henry went up there and got a job bolting on window cranks. He gets paid good money for that. Poppy's gonna work in a factory, and so am I when I'm old enough."

"No, you're not!" Poppy said emphatically. "My girls are going to school and take up typewriting. A girl can get a good job if she can type."

"I don't want a *good* job," Summer said, emphasizing *good* like it was a dirty word. "I wanna work in the factory."

"My girls are gonna learn typewriting," Poppy said again, even more emphatically.

Summer shrugged. Anderson Biddle was watching her. He was in love with her. They had met in school, and he drove up Glory Bottom two or three times a week to court her. But even though he was a town boy and got to drive his daddy's car places, Summer didn't like him *that* way. She just liked the idea of having somebody in love with her.

"So you're going away?" he said pitifully.

"What day are we leaving on?" Summer said to Poppy, ignoring Anderson Biddle.

"Around the second week in September. First I have to send seventeen dollars up front for the apartment Henry found us."

Apartment? That sounded refined. People in movies lived in apartments. I had never been in one.

"Are you coming back?" Anderson Biddle said.

"I hope not!" Summer spat out the words. "I hate this place!"

"Have you ever lived anywheres else?" Jewel said.

"You know I ain't," Summer said.

Anderson Biddle watched her some more. She was wearing a green sleeveless dress that Poppy had bought her at the company store last spring. The full skirt swirled around her prettily as she twirled around a porch post. Some people said me and Summer looked alike, and it made me so proud.

"Then how do you know you hate this place?" Ethel said crankily. "Michigan might be worse! I betcha never thought of that!"

She was acting ugly. Maybe she was mad because we were leaving and she had to stay here.

A car was snaking up the dirt road. We all stopped talking and looked to see who it was. It was the Ratliffs' car, and we reckoned that was Mr. Ratliff driving, but he was so covered up with coal dust it was hard to say for sure.

"I'm sick to death of the coal mines," Poppy said. "And it's the only living to be made in this place!"

"My daddy don't work in the mines!" Anderson Biddle said with contempt. "He owns half of the A&P!"

He had his nose stuck so far up in the air, a good rain woulda drownded him.

"Well, lah-de-dah," Jewel said. "Which half does he own?"

We all howled then, except for Poppy, and he was trying not to smile.

"Maybe he owns the half where that old clabbered milk is!" Ethel squealed with glee.

"Or the back part there where they got that withered lettuce!" Summer cracked.

Anderson Biddle was not amused.

"You can laugh," he said seriously. "But if you'd stay here, Summer, and marry me like I ast you to, it'd be half yours, too, someday."

I was wondering how many halves were in that store.

But I bit my tongue and didn't say it, 'cause Anderson Biddle had shut us all up. We waited for a response from Summer. A night owl started up. The fireflies were savoring every moment of their brief glory, just flittin' and glowin' in the summer dusk. We could barely see each other's faces. A cool breeze moved through the holler.

"She's too young to marry!" Poppy snapped. "And she's going to Michigan with me and Lyric."

"Yeah, all the way to Michigan," Summer said dreamily, as she gazed at the dark silhouettes of the hills against the sky. The pink glow was all gone by then.

"Just me and Poppy and Lyric, nobody else," she went on. "I'm not going to marry you, Anderson Biddle."

He slapped his glass of Kool-Aid down on the table, and some of it sloshed on me.

"Lookit what you did to my dress, Anderson Biddle!" I hollered at him.

He ignored me, and hissed right in Summer's face, "You'll be sorry!"

Then he left.

Ethel and Jewel giggled.

"Marry him?"

"Yeah, who'd marry him?"

Summer was quiet then. Maybe it was because she was thinking she probably wouldn't get to ride in Anderson Biddle's daddy's car anymore. Or maybe she was just give out from her big day. But I knew it wasn't because she was sorry to lose Anderson Biddle.

Drek'ly the party broke up, and Jewel switched on a flashlight she had with her so she and Ethel could see to walk down the road to their houses. They left, and we figured by this time tomorrow everybody up and down the holler would know the Comptons were moving to Flint, Michigan, come September.

Poppy went in to listen to the news on the radio. Summer stayed on the porch, and I stayed with her, but she was in no talkin' mood.

The Milky Way was shimmering, and the moon came over the mountain, round and silver as a coin. I remember how Summer watched it. Much later, when I went to my bed beside the open window, I could hear her still out there in the moonlight whispering, whispering . . .

I slept long and deep in our little house in the bottom, dreaming of things we would buy in Michigan—like lavender dresses and lace curtains.

three

for the trip we packed only our clothes, Poppy's guitar, and a few other things we couldn't part with. Poppy sold our furniture for practically nothing. Then he picked up his paycheck and we said goodbye to folks. Poppy said he had one more check coming to him, and Oliver Altizer, the clerk there at the mining company, was going to mail it to us.

We had butterflies when we left the bus depot. Shortly we were out of Virginia, and then Kentucky, where we watched the bronze-fringed mountains fall behind us. We rode through Ohio in the chilly September night, laying over in Columbus, where we ate hot dogs wrapped in warm, moist buns, and drank steaming coffee from thick white cups. We stopped in small towns where we made up stories about the people behind the doors, dreaming in their beds, unaware that the Comptons were passing through.

We fell asleep in the farmlands, and woke up with a golden sun spilling over the rim of the world. We had never seen flat land before, much less a real sunrise over a distant horizon. The three of us looked at each other with wide eyes, then back at the spectacle again, wonder-struck.

We reached Flint in mid-morning, and Henry was there to greet us. He carried us in his pickup truck to our apartment on Glenwood Avenue. Such an elegant name for a street! But it was not an elegant place to live, oh, no. We went to the second floor of a house where the Miller family with five small children lived downstairs.

Our "apartment" was a bedroom with two beds and a dresser, no closet, just a rod hung across a corner; then there was a kitchen, wallpapered with grease-splattered barnyard animals, a gas cook stove, the first Frigidaire prob'ly ever made, and a table with four mismatched chairs. Between the two rooms there was a square hallway that had a big old deep sink for washing dishes and clothes, the stairway, and a low window you could crawl out of and walk on the roof if you had a mind to. We had to go downstairs to share the bathroom with the Millers.

Our disappointment showed.

"Well, it's all I could get!" Henry said irritably. "What did y'all expect for seventeen dollars?"

"It's not for long," Poppy said to me and Summer after Henry was gone. "We'll get a bigger and better place soon's I get on at the factory. I promise."

Then he said, "You girls can have the bedroom."

He pulled the littlest bed—actually, it was a cot—into the kitchen for himself to sleep in. Me and Summer sat on the edge of the other bed, quiet for a minute; then we started hanging up our clothes on the rod in the corner.

We knew nothing about Michigan before we got there, except that it was cold, and people talked fancy. For instance, where we said, "No foolin'?" they said, "Really?" Only they didn't pronounce it *rill-y* as we did. They pronounced it *ree-al-lee*, like it had three syllables.

Now we learned some more stuff. Saginaw Street, in downtown Flint, was made out of bricks. We couldn't get over it. We wondered how many bricks it took to do that. And they had traffic lights we didn't know how to use. We stood on the street corners and looked at the lights, and some of them were red and some of them were green and some of them were yellow. We knew you had to stop on red and you could go on green, but what did you do on yellow? Then Henry told us yellow meant go real fast.

But there were lights all above the street, and we didn't know which one we were supposed to look at. It was embarrassing to stand there and watch one string of cars go, then another string, and you didn't know when to go yourself. It made you feel inferior. So we'd turn around and act like we had changed our mind about crossing the street until somebody came along who looked like they knew what they were doing. Then we followed them.

The Flint River ran behind our house, and beyond that was a Chevrolet factory. People just called it Chevrolet.

They'd say, "I work for Chevrolet," or, "That man works for Buick," or, "My brother works for Fisher Body."

That week Poppy went around to the factories putting in his application, or he went off somewhere with Henry, so he said me and Summer could postpone going to school for another week. And he let us run around the city by ourselves and get to know the place. We thought we'd died and gone to heaven. The first thing we did was find the movie theaters. There were so many of them! There was a Rialto, a Capitol, and a Palace. Each theater played a different movie every few days, and they charged you only a quarter to get in. We could walk to them, so we went to a lot of shows. There were buses all over the place, but we were used to walking, and besides, we didn't know which one to take.

Another thing we did that week was go to the Flint Centennial celebrations. The city was one hundred years old that year, and they had a lot of special events going on that week that were all free. Our favorite one was a big to-do in Atwood Stadium. Dinah Shore and her husband, George Montgomery, were there, singing and putting on the dog. We had never seen a celebrity. After the show we stood about ten feet away from Dinah Shore, but we couldn't get any closer. She was talking to some dignitaries, and rubbing Jergens lotion on her hands like an ordinary person.

They had searchlights going back and forth, back and forth across the sky over the city. We learned they were part of the celebrations, and would go on throughout the centennial year.

One evening in the lobby of this big fancy hotel called the Durant, there were tables set up with food like we'd never seen before. You could go in there and get all the free goodies you could eat, and nobody asked you who you were or what you were doing there.

It was the best week of our whole lives, and we ate more, laughed more, celebrated more, and saw more movies than all the other weeks of our life put together.

Every morning we woke up singing, and every night we went to bed humming.

And Summer said, "Do you think it'll always be this way, Lyric?"

Yes, I did.

four

but the first week ended, and we had to go to school. I joined the eighth-grade class at Zimmerman Junior High School on Corunna Road, but Summer was in the eleventh grade, and she had to go to Central. She also had to ride the city bus, and that scared her. They didn't have school buses in Flint. That was peculiar to us. We thought everybody had school buses. I was close enough to Zimmerman I could walk.

The other students at Zimmerman had been in class since Labor Day, so they were adjusted and I was the new kid.

I changed classes six times and I got lost every one of those six times. I had never changed classes before. I had four men teachers! I had never had a man teacher before. The girls had to take home economics, and the boys shop. Everybody had to take physical education, and I was told I would have to buy a blue gym suit for three dollars, and white sneakers. I already had the shoes, only we called them tennis shoes.

My homeroom teacher assigned me a locker and a combination lock, but I couldn't get it to work. I had to tell a boy my combination so he could open it for me.

When I sat down at a table by myself in the cafeteria to eat my baloney sandwich, I saw that I was the only person who brought their lunch in a poke. The others were eating baked ham with a pineapple ring and a cherry on top of it, which they bought right there in the cafeteria for thirty cents.

Some kids looked at me funny; others acted ugly to me, and a boy named Dewey even called me a name. Then a kind girl named Gladys sat down with me and tried to start a conversation. She told me her daddy was in management at Buick. He caught airplanes out at Willow Run Airport, and flew everywhere. He was gone nearly all the time, she said sadly. I figured I was lucky to have Poppy home with me every night.

I opened my mouth to say something like that, but I was so nervous the words wouldn't come out. Then I couldn't swallow my baloney sandwich, and I had to go to the bathroom to spit it out. I hoped I didn't insult her after she had been nice to me.

It was the worse day of my life, but Summer's day musta been worse than mine. When I got to the apartment I found her already there, curled up like a spring on top of the chenille bedspread. She wouldn't talk to me. Even when I told her my day was bad, too. Even when I asked her if she wanted to walk up to the drugstore on the corner and play the jukebox. Even when I told her supper was on the table. She just laid there and never said a word.

Me and Poppy ate fried potatoes, canned green beans, corn bread, and fruit cocktail for dessert. He asked me about school, and I knew I couldn't make him understand how awful it was, so I told him I'd have to get used to it. Then I told him about the gym suit.

"Tell your teacher you'll have to wait till I get my last pay from the mines," Poppy said.

"But everybody else has theirs already," I said.

"Well, I can't help it," Poppy said. "Tell your teacher what I said. Or I'll write a note. Do you want me to write a note?"

No, I didn't want him to write a note. I wanted the gym suit.

"I'll write a note. And I'll just tell her we don't have the money," Poppy said. "I'll just tell her."

It was clear when Poppy was agitated. He repeated things.

"But they won't let me take P.E. till I get the gym suit. Everybody has to have a gym suit to take P.E.," I said.

Now I was doing it, too.

"Why won't they let you take a pee?" Poppy said.

I had to laugh. And it was good to laugh. It was good to be there with Poppy where I could be the same old me I had always been. I felt better.

"Does Summer have to have a gym suit, too?" Poppy said after I explained P.E. to him.

"I don't know," I said. "Ain't she talked to you?"

"Not a word. I reckon she feels bad. First days are always bad. Tomorrow'll be better."

Poppy was right and he was wrong. School got better for me. But not for Summer.

Even though the teachers at Zimmerman Junior High didn't know my family tree clear back to its roots in England the way the teachers in Virginia did, they treated me like I was a real person anyways. Some of them even made me feel special.

My P.E. teacher smiled and put her arm around me when I gave her Poppy's note. She said it was O.K. to wait for the gym suit, and she said I could be her assistant till I got it. So I started breathing normal again that day.

Yeah, it was the teachers who saved me. But Summer was not saved. She came home the second day and went out on the roof, but there were no hills out there to talk to, only Chevrolet across the river. Finally, she came in and ate supper with us. That day we had navy beans with onions, corn bread, and milk. Poppy said tomorrow we could have pork chops.

"Don't make me go back," Summer pleaded.

"You know you have to go to school," Poppy said.

"Please don't make me," she said again. "I can get a job washing dishes at a restaurant. Henry said I could."

"You have to go to school."

"I'm sixteen. I can quit if I wanna."

"Not so long as I live and breathe."

Somehow we made it through the first week. Gladys became my friend. She was sweet. I told her about coming up from Virginia, about Summer going to Central, and about Poppy trying to get on at General Motors. Gladys introduced me to Nadine. She was a quiet, tall girl from Kentucky. Her daddy worked for Buick too, and she talked just like me.

On Friday night Summer was almost her happy self again, and we went skipping down to Saginaw Street, where they were roping off the traffic for a street dance. We bought cotton candy and strolled around amongst the people, trying to talk fancy, and acting like we had never lived anywheres else.

There was a cute boy who flirted with Summer. She fluttered her eyelids at him, and finally he asked her to dance. Away she went into the street amongst the folks. Old and young alike were dancing together on the brick pavement. I watched Summer and the boy. It was a square dance, and they twirled 'round and 'round under the streetlights, laughing and yelling "Yee-haw!" with everybody else. And I thought she was nearabout the prettiest thing there in her baby-blue dress and crinolines.

Afterwards the boy followed her around, begging for her telephone number. She didn't tell him we had no phone. She gave him an impish grin and tossed her head back. Her face was shining.

"I know you just wanna break my heart, Cutie Pie!" she said to him.

My heart swelled up with pride. That was something Bette Davis might say. Why couldn't I think of feisty things like that to say when a boy talked to me? All I could do was get tongue-tied and red in the face.

We got home late and went to the bathroom. It was right beside the Millers' kitchen. Summer stayed outside the bathroom door while I went in and turned on the light. She watched the Millers and their friends at the kitchen table where they were playing cards and drinking beer. All the young'uns were in bed, and only the grownups were at the table.

Then Summer came into the bathroom with me and closed the door. Although the cardplayers were making lots of noise when we went in, they got quiet while we were in the bathroom.

"They're listening to us," Summer whispered frantically. "They are trying to hear us go to the bathroom."

"Oh, Summer, that's silly," I said, but I was whispering, too.

About that time the Millers broke into fits of rowdy laughter.

"Three queens!" we heard Mr. Miller holler. "You had three queens all the time!"

"See?" I whispered. "They are payin' us no attention."

Poppy was already in bed, but he came out into the square hallway when he heard us. "I'm glad you're home. I was worried about you."

That was a surprise. He had never said he worried about us before.

"What're you worried for?" Summer said.

"Well," Poppy said, "I was laying there in the bed listening for you, and I got to thinking this is a big city. You don't know what might happen to young girls in big cities."

"Oh."

We had not thought of that. We had never been afraid of the night.

"Promise me you'll try to be home by dark from now on," Poppy said.

We nodded, and Poppy went back to his bed in the kitchen. I went into the bedroom and turned on the light for us. Then Summer came in and we undressed and put on our cotton nightgowns. Summer climbed into bed; then I turned out the light and got in beside her. We didn't speak again. Summer lay on her back by the window, looking at the hazy sky. Hours must have passed when I woke up to find that Summer was moving over the top of me to the other side of the bed.

"Where you goin' to?" I said sleepily.

"Shh . . . shh," she said. "I have to get away from the window."

"What for?"

"It's the searchlights," she whispered as she took my place and pushed me toward the window.

"What about 'em?"

"They're looking for me!"

Looking for her? I was too sleepy to go on with that conversation, so I rolled over and went back to sleep. The next morning when I got up, I found Summer huddled in the corner sleeping underneath the clothes rod, wrapped in a quilt.

five

Poppy's check did not come from the mining company back home. The second week of October he got on the telephone down in the Millers' living room and made the first long-distance call of his life.

He hollered into the receiver, "Oliver Altizer!"

Oliver Altizer was a town man.

"This is Claude Compton calling from up here in Flint, Michigan. Did y'all send me my last paycheck?"

"Did you leave your new address with us?" Oliver Altizer said.

" 'Course I did!" Poppy said. "I'm not addled!"

He was upset. He was broke. He had not heard from even one factory.

"I'll have to do some checking," Oliver Altizer told him.

Poppy waited.

"Well, ri'cheer it is, Claude," Oliver Altizer came back. "Did you want me to send it up there to you?"

"What do *you* think?" Poppy snapped.

Oliver Altizer said in a rather cool voice that he would

put the check in the afternoon mail. We would get it in three or four days. Three or four days? There was no money for groceries, nor even for school lunches or Summer's bus fare. We were flat busted.

"We've got flour," Poppy said, and the lines on his forehead were deep. He was worried sick. "And we've got a little milk. You can make biscuits and gravy, can't you, girls?"

I nodded. But Summer wasn't listening. She was sitting at the kitchen table, staring at her hands and laughing softly to herself. Me and Poppy looked at her, then at each other.

Then we shrugged and got back to our money problem. Back home you could just go down to the company store, and they'd give you credit till you were back on your feet.

"What about the rent?" I said. "Will the Millers wait for it?"

"They'll have to," Poppy said as he sat down heavily beside Summer. "Mrs. Miller heard me on the phone. She knows I don't have my check yet. They'll have to wait."

I was thinking about my gym suit, but I didn't mention it. I sat down, too.

"I shoulda been more careful with my spending," Poppy said wearily. "But when we left home I figgered I'd be working for GM by this time."

"How much did that phone call cost?" I said.

"I don't know," Poppy said. "I told Mrs. Miller I'd pay for it when the bill comes."

"What about Henry?" I said. "Would he loan you some money?"

"He's already loaned me money," Poppy said. "Henry's already loaned me money."

He was repeating himself again.

"Don't worry, Poppy," I said. "We'll get by somehow till you get on at a factory."

"I don't know if I'll get on," Poppy said. "That's the problem. I might not get on."

"Why do you say that?" I said. "They need people, don't they?"

"I might be too old," Poppy said. "Henry said I might be too old. They don't hire people over thirty-five 'less they have to."

Poppy was thirty-nine.

"When did he tell you that?" I said.

"The other day. The other day he said I might be too old."

"Well, how come he didn't tell you that sooner?" I hollered. "Now's a fine time to tell you, after we've come all this way. How old is Henry?"

"He's thirty-nine too, but when he came up here they were hiring people over thirty-five. Now they might not be. Henry don't know for sure."

I was mad at Henry. Why hadn't he told us? But if he had, would we have come anyway? It was hard to say.

Summer had her legs crossed, and she was swinging the top one. She was just sitting there, staring at the herbs-and-spices pattern in the oil tablecloth. And her leg kept jerking harder and faster.

"So what are we gonna do?" I said to Poppy.

"I wonder if we've made a mistake," Poppy said. "I wonder if we orta go back home."

"*No!*" Summer wailed suddenly. "We're not going back to that place! I hate that place! If you take me back, I'll kill myself!"

"You hush your mouth!" Poppy said sternly. "I don't wanna hear you sayin' such a thing as that! Besides, I figured you'd be happy to go back home, the way you hate that school."

"I'm not going back!" Summer said again.

"Back where?" I said. "Virginia or school?"

"Neither one! I'm not going back to neither one!"

She put her face in her hands and began to rock back and forth, back and forth, moaning.

"What'chu actin' like this for?" Poppy said to her.

Summer continued to rock and to moan.

The next morning Poppy said we didn't have to go to school until we had the money for lunch and bus fare. Summer lay curled into a ball in the bed, and wouldn't get up.

Me and Poppy took turns washing in the sink. He shaved and dressed in his nice blue slacks and shirt. I put on my best dress. We were going to the grocery store on the corner. It was called Hammady's. We were going to ask for credit. I knew Poppy would rather stick needles in his eyes than do that. But he had to. We had to eat.

Even though it was only October and still warm back

home, it was getting chilly in Michigan, and the radiator had been pumping out heat for more than a week. So we put on our coats, and went to the store.

"I wanna see Mr. Hammady," Poppy said to the clerk. He added "please" as an afterthought.

"Who?" the clerk said. She was just a young girl chewing bubble gum.

"Mr. Hammady, the owner. Ain't this Mr. Hammady's store?"

"Yeah, but he don't stay here. There's a whole bunch of Hammady's stores, Mister. They're all over Flint."

Poppy got red in the face.

"Then who's in charge?" he said. "At this store, I mean? Who's the boss?"

"She is!" the girl said, and pointed to a woman working at a desk in a cubicle beside the front door.

A woman? Well, I'll be dogged.

"Will you tell her I'd like to see her please?" Poppy said.

"What for?" the girl said. She blew a bubble with her gum.

I saw Poppy's face tighten at the girl's rudeness.

"Just tell her, please," he said.

"There's no work here, Mister," the girl said. "So why don'cha move on?"

"I'm not here for work," Poppy said, gritting his teeth. "Please?"

"Mrs. Stiltner!" the girl bellowed.

The woman looked up irritably from her work.

"There's a man here wants to see you!"

Stiltner? That was a back-home name. She motioned us to come over there to the cubicle. We went in. There was one chair, and Mrs. Stiltner motioned Poppy into it. I stood there beside him.

"What can I do for you?" she said wearily, removed her glasses, and rubbed the bridge of her nose.

I looked at Poppy and waited for him to speak. I could see shame casting a shadow on his features.

"My name is Claude Compton," he said. "I just come up here with my two girls from Virginia, and . . ."

"Compton?" Mrs. Stiltner said, and looked at Poppy with more interest. "I used to know some Comptons in Virginia. What part of Virginia?"

"Buchanan County," Poppy said quickly. "I used to know some Stiltners there, too. Are you from there?"

"I shore am," she said with a laugh, and easily slipped back into her mountain accent, which was just like ours.

They were both tickled to death, and started comparing notes about the people they knew. They were people I had heard Poppy talk about from his childhood, but I didn't know them myself. I relaxed. As Poppy and Mrs. Stiltner got more and more friendly and laughed some, I looked at the girl at the cash register. But she wasn't paying us any attention. She was reading a comic book.

"My husband couldn't get on at the factory when we come here," Mrs. Stiltner was saying. " 'Cause of his bad leg. He got a bad leg in the war. I couldn't get him to stay.

He left me last winter. Said he couldn't get used to the cold. So he went back to Virginia."

"You got kids?" Poppy said.

"Two boys, but they're nearabout grown now. One went with his daddy. Paul, the youngest one, he stayed with me. He's seventeen.

"I learned to type in school, so I was able to get a job with Hammady's, and I worked my way up. I like it. It's a good place to work. First I tried to get on at the factory, but they were not hiring women over thirty-five, and I'm thirty-nine."

"What about men?" Poppy said, and it looked like he was holding his breath.

"Oh, they're hiring men of all ages," Mrs. Stiltner said. "You look like a healthy man to me. You'll prob'ly get called soon."

Then they got to the part about us needing credit.

"No problem," Mrs. Stiltner said. "No problem, Mr. Compton. You just pick up what you need. You can charge it."

Then she smiled at me. "And who is this little lady?"

"This is my youngest," Poppy said. "Her name's Lyric. She's in the eighth grade."

"Well, Lyric," Mrs. Stiltner said. "You just pick out anything you want, you heah? I'm always glad to help folks from back home."

We got lots of bananas because Summer liked them, and bacon. She liked bacon, too. Then we got pinto beans and side meat, potatoes, corn meal, canned corn and tomatoes, milk and eggs, and some soap and stuff.

"Git'che some of that candy there, Lyric," Mrs. Stiltner said to me.

She had come over to the cash register when we were checking out.

"I'll take care of it," she went on. "Brenda," she turned to the girl and said, "put Lyric's candy on my account."

"Yes, ma'am," she said.

My eyes met Brenda's as I picked up the candy. She was surprised. Mrs. Stiltner was her boss, and now she was our friend. Bet Brenda wouldn't be so rude to us next time.

Summer was still in bed when we got back. It was after eleven. I went in there and tried to talk to her.

"We got bananas, Summer," I said to her. "And Poppy is going to fix eggs and bacon. I got some candy, too."

She groaned.

"Are you gonna sleep all day?" I said.

She bunched up into a tighter ball and buried her head under the pillow.

"Poppy," I said, when I went back into the kitchen. "What's wrong with her?"

"Who? Summer?" Poppy said, as he laid strips of bacon in the frying pan. "Growin' pains, I reckon."

When the check finally come, Poppy took it down to Hammady's, cashed it, and paid Mrs. Stiltner. Then he paid his other bills, gave me money for my gym suit and lunch money, and Summer lunch money and bus fare.

"I'm not going back to school," Summer said, but she took the money anyway.

"'Course you are," Poppy said. "You're going back to school tomorrow."

But Poppy was wrong. Summer did not go back to school. Poppy couldn't make her. In fact, he couldn't even make her get out of bed. She slept and slept and slept. She'd get up and eat a little bit. Then go back to bed.

Finally, Poppy said, "All right, Summer, we'll compromise. I'll let you stay home from school this year, if you'll promise to go back next year."

"But then I'll be a year behind," Summer said. "I don't want to be in class with people younger than me."

"Then get up and go to school!" Poppy shouted.

"No, I'm never going back."

Poppy sighed.

"I'm sixteen. You can't make me."

She had a point there.

The next day Summer dressed and went out and found a job washing dishes at a restaurant called Dad's. They were going to pay her fifty cents an hour plus one meal. She came home that day smiling. She was pleased with herself, and we thought now she'll be O.K. Maybe everybody wasn't supposed to go to school. Even if they make straight E's—E stood for Excellent back home—like Summer had always done. Even if they read big fat grownup books and understood every word like Summer did. Maybe she would decide to go back to school later.

The day after that, Poppy was hired at the Chevrolet factory, a part of General Motors, and it was a time of celebration. We could relax. His job was bolting on rearview mirrors. They put him on the second shift, which was two in the afternoon till eleven at night.

"Y'all will have to be here alone in the evenings," he said to me and Summer. "You'll have to fix supper, and look after yourselves. You'll have to call on the Millers if you have any troubles."

"That's fine, Poppy," I said to him. "We can manage."

But Summer was not listening. Once again she was sitting at the kitchen table rocking back and forth, back and forth. She was laughing low to herself, and it looked like she was tickled by the figures in the wallpaper.

six

Me and Summer and Poppy were only three out of thousands of people who came to Flint from the South that year. In their rattletrap cars and trucks they came, packed tight with their two to six young'uns and everything they owned that was any 'count. Or they came like we did on a bus, with everything in a few suitcases. All of us to seek our fortunes.

The Southern people gravitated to the same neighborhoods where you could rent cheap apartments or houses. We huddled together like farm animals in the cold, seeking warmth, comfort, and familiarity with their own kind.

By the time we got there, the stores were already stocked—by popular demand—with dried beans and corn meal, side meat and molasses. They had tons of grits too, but we had never had a bite of grits in our lives, which other Southern folks thought was peculiar. But it was the truth. We had never even seen grits before.

We learned to wear gloves and boots, scarves and earmuffs. We learned to read bus schedules and traffic lights. And we learned to be in the house by five o'clock before the evening fell so dark and cold.

Lives were planned around General Motors. Poppy could count on some days off at Christmas. And two weeks for the changeover at the beginning of July. That's when they'd be setting up the assembly lines for the new models. Maybe we would go back home for a visit with the kinfolks then, Poppy said.

He got double time for working Sundays and holidays. And triple time for working a holiday that fell on a Sunday. He was going to try and work on special days like that. Payday came every other Friday, and that's when you'd see the factory families coming out of their burrows to fight the cold for a while, to buy groceries or shop for bargains.

Where back in the South you might hear, "Are you Republican?" "Are you Baptist?", in Michigan you'd hear, "Are you Union?" And just about everybody was. Poppy became Union, too. The UAW—United Auto Workers— was one of the most powerful unions in the world, he said, and it made a man feel like he had some control over his life to belong. He had to pay dues and go to meetings and fight for more benefits.

In early November two cute young fellers from the Millers' hometown in Louisiana, just discharged from the army, rented the bedroom in the basement. They were trying to get on at a factory, too. Now twelve people lived in the house on Glenwood Avenue.

"We're leaving here soon's I find us another place," Poppy said. "This house is gittin' too crowded."

But there was a housing shortage.

Back home, if you needed a place to live, you just went out and chopped down some trees and built a couple of rooms on the side of the hill that belonged to some of your kinfolks. They might charge you for it and they might not. But if they did, you only had to pay a few dollars for steep land. If it was *real* steep, you could put some stilts under your house. Over the years you'd add a room here, a room there, a bathroom if you were lucky. And eventually you'd have a pretty good place.

But in Flint, Michigan, you couldn't do that. First of all, there was something already built on practically every patch of land in sight. Second, you couldn't chop down a tree. They were all in somebody's yard. And third, you had to have a thing called a building permit even to tack a porch on to your place.

There was an article in the *Flint Journal* about people taking advantage of the poor moving up from the South, charging them high rent for practically nothing, and putting too many people in a house. They didn't say anything about people from the South, like the Millers, taking advantage of their own kind. Until then I had not realized we were poor. We had never seemed poor before, but now I could see where it might look that way to Yankees.

Summer was happy with her job, and with the money she was making. She took a fancy to one of the ex-soldiers in the basement. His name was Bill. When she got off work, she hung around outside in the cold, just to see him come and go. When she saw him, she flirted with him, and he talked to her, but he didn't ask her for a date. I heard him tell his buddy he knew better than to date young girls.

"Yeah, 'cause her daddy would prob'ly kill you!" the other feller said with a chuckle.

I told Summer what I heard, but she didn't give up. She started spending all her money from Dad's on lipstick and makeup and new dresses.

Then her face broke out. Summer had always been fair-complected, but now the pinkness turned to red and was covered with pimples. She was frantic.

"Oh, no," she wailed in front of the mirror over the sink. "Just look at me. I'm ugly! I'm so ugly!"

"Will you quit pickin' at it!" Poppy hollered at her. "Just leave it alone, and stop that moanin' and groanin'. Dab some Noxzema on your face every night, and quit pickin' at it, and it'll be all right. Your mama used Noxzema from the time she was sixteen till the day she died and she never had a pimple—not the first one."

So Summer used Noxzema every night, but she couldn't stop picking at her face. She'd pick a place till it bled, and natur'ly you're gonna keep sores on your face if you can't leave them alone.

"I can't help it!" she told Poppy. "I forget. I start thinking about something, and I forget what I'm doing. It's just a habit."

She was right about that. I watched her. At night she sat

by the window not doing anything, just sitting there, sometimes with a secret smile on her face, and swinging her leg,
faster and harder, and picking at her face. It got worse and
worse. It got so bad she stopped going out a'tall. She was
afraid Bill might see her. She went back to bed and stayed
there. After a few days of this, the restaurant called Mrs.
Miller's house, and somebody hollered up the stairs.

"Summer Compton! You up there?"

But Summer didn't answer. She hid her head down under the covers and wouldn't even peep out.

"Summer Compton! Dad's called and wanted to know if
you are coming back to work."

"Tell them no," I answered for Summer. "She's sick."

Somebody downstairs snorted. "Sick, my hind end!"

Dad's didn't call again, and Summer's last paycheck was
mailed to her. She didn't work anywhere after that.

I got the bright idea of putting thin cotton gloves on
Summer's hands so she wouldn't forget and pick at her
face. And she said it was O.K. She wore the gloves all the
time, and her face began slowly to heal, but she had scars.
Her days of pretty complexion were over.

seven

At school we had debates in Social Studies class about integration. I didn't know what that word meant till I listened to the debates for a while. Then I figured it out.

What surprised me was that my classmates were all saying they did not want to go to school with colored children. No matter where they were raised, they said that. Some had lived in Michigan all their lives.

They said, "I'm not prejudiced, *but* I think we should be separate but equal." Or, "I'm not prejudiced, *but* I think they should have their own neighborhoods and their own schools."

And I had always figured up-North folks were so open-minded. In fact, before I came here, I had thought all the schools and neighborhoods would be mixed. But I was wrong. There were no colored children in Zimmerman Junior High, nor even in our neighborhood.

I didn't join the debates, because I was too bashful. I just listened. But I did have some opinions of my own, and I debated in my head.

Everybody talked about the South like it was brimming over with colored folk, and you couldn't go anywhere without running into one. Actually, in my whole life I had not seen a colored person in the flesh until I was on my way to Flint. Still, I knew in my heart of hearts that colored folks were just like me, no better and no worse. I don't know how I knew. I just did. They were people like me.

And I figured when people say, "I'm not prejudiced, *but* . . . ," that means they really *are* prejudiced, and they are just trying to find a way to make it O.K. So I would say to myself I am *not* prejudiced, and there's no *but*s about it.

I decided I would tell the class all of that one of these days. But when the teacher, Mr. Pinkney, finally did call on me for my opinion, I couldn't speak. I just turned red, and looked at my hands and felt their eyes on me for what seemed like a long, long time, until finally he moved on to somebody else.

Then Mr. Pinkney talked to us about how important it is to think for yourself and not be influenced by the attitudes of other people, no matter who they are. He said you shouldn't never accept what somebody says just 'cause they said it. You should question things.

"Other people's attitudes sometimes seep into our thoughts by osmosis," he went on, and we all knew what that meant, 'cause we'd been reading about osmosis in Science. "We absorb them, and we start to think these are our own thoughts. That's how, if we're not alert, we let other people do our thinking for us. And unscrupulous people can get control of our minds in that way."

After class that day a girl named Yolanda came up to me at my locker, where I was whirling the dial on my combination lock like I'd been doing it all my life. She was a dark-haired beauty. She had what they call "snapping black eyes" in *True Story Magazine*, perfect straight teeth, and rosy cheeks. In fact, I had eyed her lots of times when she didn't know it, and I had thought that's what I would pick to look like if I had a choice in the matter.

"You don't feel that way about colored people, do you?" she asked.

I shook my head.

"Me neither," she said.

It was the beginning of our friendship, and I was thrilled that a girl like Yolanda would be friendly with me. Our walk home took us in the same direction.

"My mama is dead, too," she told me. "My daddy and me, we came up here from Texas last year."

I reckoned her Southern drawl was worse than mine.

"Do you remember your mama?" I asked.

"Oh, yeah, she only died two years ago."

"I don't remember my mama, but I wisht I did," I said.

"I'll tell you a secret," Yolanda said and put her lips near my ear. "Promise you won't tell?"

"Sure," I agreed.

You'd think we'd been buddies for years.

"My mama was a colored woman," she whispered.

"Then how come you ain't colored?" I said.

"She was *half* colored. Her daddy was white, and her

mama was colored. And my own daddy is full-blooded Mexican. I take after him. I don't tell everybody 'bout Mama 'cause they start treatin' me different soon's they find out. And you know something, Lyric? They peck you to death when you're different."

I just looked at her.

"Back in Texas, I usta have chickens. They were just your ordinary run o' the mill, cluckin', squawkin', egg-layin' chickens, you know? But I liked 'em.

"And then this solid white one come along. I called her Opal. She was so pretty. But the other chickens ganged up on Opal and pecked, pecked, pecked at 'er. They woulda killed her too, if I hadn't took up for her."

What she was saying that day, I didn't get right then, and I didn't know what to say. So I didn't say anything, 'cause I had learned from reading Mark Twain that it's better to keep your mouth shut and appear stupid, than to open it and remove all doubt. I had been reminded of that lesson quite often since coming to Michigan.

"I can go down Glenwood Avenue with you," she offered when we were nearing our parting of the ways. "Then I can cut over to West Court. That's where I live."

But I didn't want her to see our house. I was afraid she might drop in sometime, and I was ashamed of the apartment. I would ask her over when Poppy found us a better place to live.

"Oh, I have to stop at the drugstore today," I lied, "and pick up some things for Poppy."

And I thought I was saved.

But she said, "I'll go to the drugstore with you."

"O.K.," I said lamely. "Don't your daddy expect you home?"

"He's on the second shift. Nobody's home."

"Same here," I said.

Somewhere in the back of my head I wondered why I had said that. Summer was home. She was somebody. Was I ashamed of her, too?

We went into the drugstore at the corner where West Court and Glenwood came together, and I moved around amongst the shelves, thinking I would buy some lil' ole something we needed, but it would have to be *real* little, 'cause I didn't have much money with me.

"Wanna get a soda?" Yolanda said.

"Sure," I agreed, and we went to the counter, perched upon the stools, and told the soda jerk to give us fountain cherry Cokes.

He was a young feller. And he was plainly smitten with Yolanda. He couldn't keep his eyes off of her.

"Wanna play the jukebox?" Yolanda said to me, not paying him a bit of attention.

"Sure," I agreed again, and we went over to the jukebox to see what they had.

"I just love this one," Yolanda said, and she punched "Moments to Remember" by the Four Lads.

We sat back down and listened. It had the sweetest harmony, which Yolanda appreciated as much as I did. It also had pretty words, which I memorized.

Though summer turns to winter
And the present disappears
The laughter we were glad to share
Will echo through the years.

Then we played another song and sipped on our drinks, and talked some more. The soda jerk got to talking to us, nobody else came into the store, and I was happy. It smelled like vanilla extract in there, and it was so cozy and cheerful I lost track of the time.

When I looked out and saw how dark it was, I like to died. Summer was alone with nobody to turn on a light for her!

"Oh, Yolanda!" I said. "I gotta go! It's dark out there!"

"Yeah, it gets dark so early nowadays," she said. "But what about your daddy's stuff you were supposed to get?"

"It can wait," I mumbled. "I gotta go."

And I rushed out and down the street.

As I got up close to the house I could see a flickering glow in the kitchen. What could that be? I hurried up the stairs calling Summer's name. I was breathing so fast.

"I'm here, Summer! I'm home!"

"In the kitchen, Lyric!" she called out excitedly. "Come see!"

The flickering I had seen from the street was coming from a candle. Summer had perched it and lit it in the middle of the table, and she was standing there over it.

"What'chu doin'?" I said.

"Oh, look, Lyric! See how big I am!"

She was bending her body up and down, up and down over the candle, and the light threw a creepy black shadow of her all over the room. The shadow was normal-sized when she moved away from the candle, but when she got closer to the light, it loomed up bigger and bigger until it covered the whole ceiling and the walls.

"I am a giant!" she squealed. "Lookit! Lookit! I am big! The candle makes me so big!"

I was relieved she wasn't upset. I tossed my books on Poppy's cot and watched her move back and forth, back and forth again and again, giggling and clapping her hands like a little girl.

"I am big, Lyric! I am big!"

And I had a sudden memory of me and Summer at the county fair two or three years ago, and we were riding on the Ferris wheel. We were both so happy that day.

Eating cotton candy high over a crowd of mountain people, Summer had looked down at them and squealed, "See how little they are, Lyric! They look like ants, and we are big! We are *so* big!"

eight

A few days later, when I got home, Summer was not laughing. She was pacing, pacing, pacing in the kitchen.

"It's about time you got here," she said to me real hateful. "I been all by myself again. It's Poppy's day off and he went someplace with that Stiltner woman from the store!"

"Mrs. Stiltner?" I said. I was tickled. "Well, ain't that something? Did you see her?"

"No, he was meeting her at the store."

Summer went on pacing. Back and forth. Back and forth. From the window to the door and back again. It was about eight steps.

"He shouldn't be courtin'!" she said hotly, and folded her arms across her chest.

"Why not?" I said. "I think it's nice."

"No!" Summer said and stomped her foot hard on the kitchen floor. "No, it's *not* nice!"

"What's wrong with it?" I said. "Mrs. Stiltner's man left

her. They been separated a year now. She's thirty-nine years old, and so's Poppy. He ain't had a girlfriend since Mama died, and . . ."

"Mama is *not* dead!" Summer screamed.

The most peculiar thing was not what she said but how she said it. She made the words come out shrill and loud, but the expression on her face didn't change, and she didn't fling her arms around or anything. It seemed like the sound came from somebody else, maybe a monster, way down deep inside her, and she had nothing to do with it.

The scream echoed in the room as I took some cold biscuits, parked at the table, and started nibblin'. I didn't have much of an appetite. I was thinking of all the idiotic things Summer had done since we got to Michigan. Yeah, I thought, *idiotic* was the word, but it was that bloodcurdling scream of hers that gave me goose bumps.

Mama is not dead? I faced it right then. Something was bad wrong with Summer. She stood there for a moment perfectly still. Then she went back to pacing, and babbling.

"I told him. I told him not to go. I told him you'd be mad. I told him. I did my part. Jibble, jibble."

Jibble, jibble?

I watched her. Her face was better, but not normal yet. Her hands were bare, but during the time she had been wearing the gloves, she'd let her fingernails grow out. Now they were awful long and dirty. She had on a ratty old housecoat, and her hair was hanging in her face in dirty strands. She hadn't washed it or even combed it for some time.

Seeing her every day I had not noticed what a great big change this was from her old self. But if somebody from back home saw Summer right then, I'll declare they wouldn't have even recognized her as that same bright-eyed little gal she usta be. They might have even thought she was some crazy woman.

"He won't listen to me. You'll have to tell him. When he comes home, jibble, you tell him," she went on.

I spoke up then. "You talking to me, Summer?"

"No!" she screamed. "You stay out of this. It's none of your business."

"Then who're you talking to?"

"Mama!" she screamed again. "I was telling Mama what Poppy's done! Don't you know that? Oh, he thought he could get away with this! But he can't. I told!"

"Summer," I said. "Where is Mama?"

"She's ri'cheer, Lyric!" Summer said and pointed to the air in front of her. She said it like I was slow in the head, and she had lost patience with me. "Right beside Grandpa!"

I would have laughed then if she hadn't been so pathetic.

"Grandpa?" I said. "He's not dead either?"

"Yeah," Summer said more calmly as she sat down beside me. "Yeah, Grandpa's dead, jibble, jibble."

"Summer, what do you mean by that . . . that jibble?"

"Jibble, jibble," she said.

"Jibble is not a word, Summer."

"It is my word, Lyric—*my* word," she went on. "It is not yours! And you know what else? It was that foreman's fault, jibble. Grandpa told me if that foreman hadn't a'said what he did, well, you know, Grandpa might've lived."

It was funny she should say that. I had often thought of it myself, but never would I mention such a thing out loud. I hadn't heard anybody else say it either. That foreman could very well have made a mistake in his calculations. And if he hadn't told those miners they had only one hour to live, then our grandpa might've been rescued right along with the others.

"I think that's the truth," I said seriously to Summer. "That foreman was just an educated idiot who orta kept his mouth shut. Then everybody—including Grandpa—could've gone on hoping."

Summer seemed satisfied with that. She sat at the table with me while I ate, and she didn't talk to Mama anymore. But she didn't talk to me either. I tried to say things about school, but her mind was somewheres else again, and after a while she got up and left the room right in the middle of my talking. Then I could hear her in the bedroom whispering, whispering . . . jibble, jibble . . .

I decided it was time for me and Poppy to have a serious talk about this stuff Summer was doing. He came home about nine, smelling of cooked onions and tobacco. Summer was in bed. I was sitting at the kitchen table studying. He kissed me on top of my head.

"What'chu learnin'?" he said.

"The minor keys," I said.

"The whichum?" he said and looked at my music book, which was open in front of me.

"The Michigan kids have been studying music theory all the years they've been in school," I said. "And I was way behind, but I'm almost up with them now."

"I never learned any of that stuff," Poppy said as he picked up his guitar. "But it never stopped me from playing any song I heard."

"Yeah, but most folks can't do that, Poppy."

Softly he began to pluck out the notes to "Wildwood Flower."

"Have fun tonight?" I said.

"It was all right. I met Gayle's boy, Paul. He's a right nice young feller."

Poppy began to sing.

> *I'll twine 'mid the ringlets of my raven black hair*
> *With the roses so red and the lilies so fair*
> *The myrtle so green of an emerald hue*
> *The pale morning glory with eyes of bright blue.*

That song always brought dreamy images to my mind. I could see that sad-eyed little thing way back there in the hills a long time ago. Maybe she was one of the first settlers in the Appalachians, except for the Indians. Or maybe *she* was Indian, 'cause she talks about her raven-black hair. Anyhow, she's sitting there alone in a deep holler, plaiting wildflowers into her long hair, and this song comes to her mind, born from her grief and longing. She never imagined it would echo its way down through the generations.

I added my alto to Poppy's baritone melody.

> *He taught me to love him, and promised to love*
> *Through ill and misfortune, all others above*
> *But I woke from my dreaming, my idol was clay*
> *My visions of love have all faded away.*

> *I'll think of him never, I'll be wildly gay*
> *I'll charm every heart, and drive troubles away*
> *I'll live yet to see him regret this dark hour*
> *When he won and neglected his frail wildwood flower.*

Our pleasant song suddenly ended in discord and racket as Poppy let out a cry and tossed his treasured guitar onto the floor with a loud ker-boom and an echo of vibrating strings.

My eyes went to the doorway where Poppy was looking. Summer was standing there in her nightgown with bloody scratches on her face. We both rushed to her side.

"Oh, my darlin' girl!" Poppy said. "What's happened to you?"

"See what they did to me," she said softly.

"Summer, what happened?" I cried out.

"They scratched me. They wanted to taste my blood," she said, still calm and controlled.

"Who? What on earth do you mean?" Poppy said.

"The wolves were here," Summer said. "They did this to me."

Me and Poppy were stunned. We couldn't even move for a few seconds, then we sprung into action at the same time.

"Come sit at the table," Poppy said, as he led her there.

I got a clean cloth and dabbed at her wounds. I could see that the scratches were not very deep, but one had grazed the corner of her right eye.

Summer just sat there, serene and still at last, with the palms of her hands turned upward on her knees. You could see the blood layered above the dirt underneath her long fingernails.

"Go down and ask the Millers to fetch a doctor for us," Poppy said quietly to me.

And I scurried down the stairs.

But in Michigan you couldn't fetch a doctor to save your life. You had to go to him. The Millers told me that and followed me back up the stairs.

"Did you call the doctor?" Poppy said, when we entered the kitchen. He was sitting by Summer with one arm around her.

"What happened?" Mr. Miller said.

"She hurt her eye," Poppy said. "Is the doctor coming or not?"

"Doctors don't come to you here, but we'll take her to the emergency room for you," Mrs. Miller said.

"Oh," Poppy said. "All right." Then he turned to me. "Get her coat, will you, Lyric? And her shoes."

I rushed into our room, found Summer's coat, shoes, and socks and returned to the kitchen. Then me and Poppy put on Summer's things for her, while she just sat there, limp and dazed, still in her nightgown under the coat. When I looked at the Millers again, I found them in the same position, staring at Summer. They didn't know what to say.

Poppy put his own coat back on, and we led Summer down the stairs. The Millers got together their coats and car keys while me and Poppy huddled with Summer at the front door. Then the grownups led her out to the car.

Nobody said it, but I knew it was my place to stay with the Miller children, who were sleeping. I stood at the front window, clutching the ledge and looking after the car long after it was out of sight.

They treated Summer's wounds, then put her in the psychiatric ward at Hurley Hospital and kept her there for three days before they let anybody see her. Poppy paced the floor and acted about as crazy as Summer. He blamed his own self for what happened, saying if he'd stayed home with her she'd be all right.

"I won't leave her alone no more," he said.

But in all our years together I couldn't remember Poppy ever neglecting us in any way. This was not his fault. So I tried to tell him that. Still he beat up on himself.

"I knew she wadn't acting right, and I had no business traipsing off to have a good time," he said.

When Poppy was allowed to see her, I couldn't go with

him. It was no place to take a thirteen-year-old girl, they said.

Poppy was even more shook up after he saw Summer. He said it really was the awfullest place, and he couldn't hardly stand to see his sweet girl left there. He said people were screamin' and cussin', and some of them were in straitjackets 'cause you couldn't turn 'em loose. But Summer just lay there, very still, and she didn't seem to care about anything.

They had forced her into a hot bath, Poppy told me, where they had cut her fingernails, and also cut her hair real short and washed it. Then they had put her in a white hospital gown, treated the eye, and dabbed some purple medicine on her face, but didn't bandage it. They had to tie her hands to the bed to keep her from picking at the scratches.

"I never seed anything so pitiful in my life," Poppy said with a quiver in his voice. "It didn't look like our Summer a'tall. And if her name hadn't been on the bed chart, I wouldn't a'known who it was."

He was so hurt and sad, I'll declare I don't know how Poppy went on working, but he felt like he had to. He said his girls needed him to keep on working now more than ever.

"They're saying Summer thinks things are after her. And she's got delusions and hallucinations," Poppy told me. "She thinks she sees the dead. She's gone mental, and that's all there is to it."

"Couldn't they tell you something we didn't already know?" I said, not meaning to be sarcastic. But it was the truth.

"The mind is a complicated and mysterious thing, Lyric, my girl. And I'll declare, as good as the doctors are, I don't think they know a lot about it."

Then he put his head in his hands and said a prayer of thanks to Jesus for General Motors and that good hospitalization policy they gave him. Because, otherwise, what on earth would become of his Summer?

"They've put her on some real powerful medicine," he went on, "and she's calmed down for now."

nine

On December 23, Poppy brought Summer home—a zombie. She gave me a shadow of a smile when she first came in, but she didn't smile again for a spell. You could see the red streaks all down her face where she had scratched herself. Her right eye had a big blood spot in the white part. Her fingernails were short, but I put the white gloves back on her anyway, and she didn't object.

She took her pills like she was supposed to, then she sat there in the kitchen and looked out the window. The medicine made her sluggish, and she moved in slow motion.

I fixed meals, and she ate when I called her to the table. She spoke hardly at all, and when she did, her speech was slow. Her words came out slurred like she couldn't get her mouth open wide enough to make the right sounds. She told me when she needed to go to the bathroom, and most times I went with her, not just to turn on the light, but because she seemed so helpless.

———

On Christmas Eve, heavy gray snow clouds gathered all day and dumped their load by nightfall. And such a snow! A stark white beauty transformed Glenwood Avenue, covering the shabbiness. It was a miracle out there under the streetlamps.

Summer sat by the window and watched. I kept thinking, *Silent night, holy night . . .*

I carried a cup of cocoa to her on a saucer. "Want a marshmallow?" I asked softly, placing the saucer into her hands.

"No."

I sat down with her. With our heads together we sipped and looked out at the cold night, wordless.

Indoors, it was not a Christmas you would dream about. No stockings hung over the fireplace. We didn't have a fireplace. Not even a chimney. No excited previous days full of shopping and planning. No breathless whispered secrets and giggles. No decorations on the front porch, which wasn't even ours to decorate. No reindeer. I remembered Christmases back home when we had all of those things, and I felt an ache around my heart.

Poppy had given me a few dollars, which I had spent hurriedly at the drugstore one evening before darkness fell. There were a few presents under a pitiful tree in the corner. A few goodies in the ancient refrigerator, and on the table. Only a hope and a promise that this was temporary. Next year would be better. That was the gift we gave to each other.

Next year we'll live in a house, I thought.

Next year we'll have a big tree with lights.

And presents and a ham.

Next year she'll be well again.

Poppy was out doing some last-minute shopping with Henry. He had promised to be home by eight. Earlier in the evening we'd eaten a small supper I had fixed. In Michigan you didn't have to buy a whole turkey. You could buy only a part. So that's what we did. We had bought a small breast of turkey, and cranberry sauce in a jar. I had made gravy, biscuits, and mashed potatoes, and heated up canned green beans. We had store-bought pumpkin pie, and it was good. We had all eaten until we were stuffed, even Summer.

"When is Poppy coming home?" she asked now.

Again she sounded like a child.

"Soon."

Some people were strolling down the sidewalk in the snow, singing carols.

"That's a tradition here," I said to Summer. "People go up and down the street singing carols on Christmas Eve."

You couldn't do that back home, I was thinking. In the hollers there was no good place to walk. And you didn't have any lights. You were liable to fall down the creek bank in the dark. And the houses were too far apart. You might have to walk for miles. Yeah, caroling was definitely a city tradition.

"Maybe we could do it next year," Summer said.

"Yeah, we can," I said brightly. "We'll plan on it."

We watched the snow some more.

"Remember that movie we saw last year?" I said. "The one with Bing Crosby? *White Christmas*?"

She turned to me then with that ghost of a smile. "Yeah, I remember."

"Remember the song we learned—'Sisters'?"

"Yeah, I do."

"Let's sing it now."

"O.K."

We played around with the notes for a minute, trying to find the right key. Then it came.

> *Those who've seen us*
> *Know there's not a thing*
> *Can come between us!*

It felt so right to sing in harmony with her again. Her words came out more distinct when she sang, and her voice was as good as ever, which was far better than most folks'.

> *Lord, help the mister*
> *Who comes between me and my sister!*
> *And Lord help the sister*
> *Who comes between me and my man!*

"Let's do a Christmas carol now," she said then.

"O.K., which one?"

"*When flowers blossomed mid the snow . . .*" she sang in her clear high voice, so like a bell, and I joined in with my alto.

> *. . . Upon a winter's night,*
> *Was born a child, the Christmas rose,*
> *The king of love and light!*

After that, we sang some more songs before Poppy came home. We could hear his footsteps on the stairs, and we began to sing "Lo, How a Rose E'er Blooming." It was his favorite. He took off his coat and boots. He had an air of cold about him. His cheeks were red and his hands were chapped, and he rubbed them together.

He placed two beautifully wrapped presents under the tree real careful, then stood there smiling at us as we sang in that dingy little kitchen. I knew his heart was full at seeing Summer singing again, and I knew he was thinking about us—his girls. His songbirds, as he usta call us. His life. We always knew we were loved. Always.

Just stood there, he did, and listened to us sing on Christmas Eve, as the snow threw a merciful blanket over us, and gave us this bittersweet Christmas together.

ten

beginning the first of January, Summer went to see a psychiatrist every Tuesday and Friday morning at eleven o'clock. That was right when I went to Mr. Buell's English class, and I would look at the clock on the wall and think of her, and wonder what she was saying to the doctor.

Was she talking about our life together way back there in the bottom between the hills? Was the doctor seeing into that head of hers and figuring out what made her go mental? We had the same childhood. Did they know how come she had so much fear in her that I didn't have? What was it that haunted her so?

There was such a big sadness in our Summer that you couldn't even comprehend the depth of it. I would ask her about her visits to the doctor, but she didn't want to talk about it. I kept thinking of the Bible verse, *"Yea, though I walk through the valley of the shadow of death . . ."* It seemed like that was where my sister was at—in the valley of the shadow of death. And when I remembered the happy-birthday face from last August—only five months ago—I wondered if I would ever see it again.

One night I had a strange dream.

Me and Summer are walking up Glory Bottom. We are barefooted. It is dark and we are afraid, so we hurry, holding on to each other. The holler is deeper, colder, more isolated than I remember it ever being. The hills are taller, the woods thicker. Rolling purplish black clouds are moving in the sky over us. Moving, moving, rumbling . . . rumbling . . .

"We'll be home soon, Summer," I whisper. "Hold on to me."

And then there are green eyes in the dark behind us. And there are huge paws hitting heavy on the packed-down dirt, and there are panting sounds. It's wolves after us, big black wolves with long sharp teeth, nipping at our heels.

"Run, Summer! Run!"

And we run together, unable to see the road, not knowing how close we are to the creek bank. And suddenly I sprout wings, and I lift myself up a few feet off the road. Still I hold on to Summer.

"Come on, Summer, fly!"

"I can't. I can't fly! I can't get my feet off the ground!"

"Sure you can. It's easy. Just jump up into the air like this."

And I am flying, flying, but I am still holding on to Summer, trying to help her lift off. The wolves are closing in. We can hear them growling and feel their hot breath.

"Don't leave me, Lyric! Please don't leave me behind!"

But I am terrified. I let go of Summer. I let go and I fly away.

I woke up with a cry.

Oh, Summer, Summer, I had to let go . . .

Our bedroom was very dark. I looked out at the night sky and tried to calm my racing heart. I could hear Summer's deep breathing beside me.

"Thank you, God, it's not real. Thank you, God, it was only a dream."

It was that kind of dream. That kind of feeling. Just too awful to dwell on, so you try to forget it.

At breakfast Poppy asked Summer in his quiet way how she had slept, and she said, "I had a bad dream."

"A nightmare?" Poppy said gently.

"Yeah, a nightmare. The wolves again," she said, and her voice was tiny and weak like a child's. "In Glory Bottom, they were after me."

"And what happened?" I said, holding my breath.

"I don't remember," she said. "I just don't remember. But I don't want to talk about it no more."

I did a lot of thinking about that, and I couldn't explain it, but I felt that maybe me and Summer had dreamed the same dream again. Only I remembered how it ended. And I figured God had given me this little bitty taste of Summer's terror so I'd understand. And I did understand. I understood that she was in a nightmare she couldn't wake up from.

eleven

At school I learned to say "ree-al-lee," and "yous guys" instead of "y'all." Don't ask me why yous guys is more proper than y'all. I don't know.

I learned not to jump out of my desk and run to the window when an airplane flew over so low you could read the numbers on the wings. I had done that once, saying, "Looky yonder, would'ja?" And for some reason I thought everybody else would jump up too, but I was wrong.

Dewey the heckler had said, "Hillbilly, hillbilly," low under his breath as I went back to my seat with a red face. So I learned to ignore planes that acted like they wanted to land on the roof, even if I was itching to go see.

I had learned not to say, "I'm give out," after running laps around the gym. And I had also learned not to say "Tarnation!" when somebody told what the temperature was, even though I had never before seen the mercury in a thermometer drop so low.

The cold was bitter and brutal. It got way down in your bones, and you couldn't get away from it.

By the time I walked to Zimmerman from home, that bare place on my legs between the top of my boots and the hem of my dress was numb. Girls were not allowed to wear slacks to school. It made me mad to be so cold when I could look around me and see the boys had their legs all covered up in corduroy or wool, warm as toast.

"What's the problem with slacks?" I said angrily to Yolanda, Gladys, and Nadine as we were going into Mrs. Gaspar's first-period music class one morning. We four had become pretty good friends by then. "I can't feel my legs!"

"It's not ladylike," Gladys said sarcastically.

"Well, it's not ladylike to freeze your legs off either!" I said.

"No, 'cause then you have to walk around on your butt!" Yolanda said.

My mad spell evaporated as we all busted out laughing. Mrs. Gaspar tried to call the class to order, but we were hysterical.

"What's so funny?" she said, but we couldn't even speak. "Lyric, see me after class. Maybe you can find your voice by then."

Just Lyric? What was fair about that? Now I was mad again. Seeing Mrs. Gaspar after class probably meant detention. I had it all planned how I would tell her she was unfair. How come she picked me out of that group of four?

But when I went up to her desk after class with all that rebellion puffing me up, she knocked the wind out of my sails.

"You know I don't want you to make a habit of this, Lyric, but it's good to see you laughing. You usually seem sad."

Nobody had ever told me that before. Back home, folks said I could light up a room. But maybe it was not so anymore. I didn't know what to say.

"Are you homesick?" she went on.

I thought about it.

"Once in a while," I replied.

"What do you miss most?" Mrs. Gaspar said, giving me her complete and undivided attention. She was a pretty lady, with nice blond hair and blue eyes. She played the piano, and she knew everything there was to know about music.

"I guess I miss Summer the most," I said wistfully.

And that was double-talk. Only Mrs. Gaspar didn't know it.

"Oh, the cold weather makes you feel sad?" she said kindly.

I shrugged and said, "Not sad exactly. But I can't help remembering how things usta be."

I thought the world and all of Mrs. Gaspar, and she wasn't just nodding her head and thinking of other things like some teachers do. She was really listening to me; but somehow I just couldn't tell her about Summer.

After a little while she gave me a pass for my next class so I wouldn't get a tardy mark, and I went on.

I realized that somewheres back in those hills I had absorbed this attitude—like Mr. Pinkney's osmosis—that insanity was one of those skeletons you wanted to keep in the closet.

I remembered the Moore family who lived way high on a mountaintop. They had a crazy aunt who sat in a rocking chair on the porch all the time and hollered out nasty things. They called her Sadie. If somebody chanced to go by the house, which was not too often, they jerked Sadie inside and closed the door. When you did something dumb, folks were apt to call you Sadie.

Then there was Billie Shell. He was really nutty. They kept him hid as long as they could, but they finally had to send him off to the lunatic asylum.

And I thought of all the sayings people have for the mentally ill. Words I had picked up myself. Crazy. Nuts. She's got a screw loose. He lost his marbles. Batty. Lunatic. Looney.

That day after school I went to the grocery store because there were things we needed and couldn't do without another day. Like soap and potatoes. Sure, I got some pop too, but I was there anyways, and I wouldn't have gone just for pop. I wouldn't have gone just for the Cracker Jacks either. And I did get Summer some bananas. So I really was thinking of her.

I hurried as fast as I could, but it got dark on me before I could get home. I rushed up the steps, hauling groceries and calling for Summer. I lost my breath doing it, but she was not in the apartment!

I dumped my pokes on the table. I was scared to death. Where was she? I had heard Poppy make her promise she wouldn't go anywhere from the time he went to work till I got home. When I came straight from school, it was not a long time for her to sit beside the window and wait, like she promised she would.

With my heart flying, I went running down the stairs again. The Millers were out, and the house seemed empty and spooky. It echoed. I found her standing right outside the bathroom in the dark in a puddle. She had wet herself.

"I wanted to go in and turn on the light all by myself," she said in her tiny voice. She sounded like a mouse squeaking. "I was determined. It wasn't all the way dark then, but . . . but I couldn't, Lyric. I was too skeerd to go in and flip on the switch. I froze up."

So she had stood outside the door, and couldn't move. But she couldn't hold it in either.

I thought about her wanting to go in the bathroom and turn on the light by herself. She had never done that before, and it was like something inside her was telling her it was a matter of life and death, but still she couldn't do it.

My mind went to those happy Saturdays back home, sitting in a dark movie theater with Summer. There was a particular scene we had seen maybe fifty times in different movies. You know the one where somebody is hanging off a cliff or a window ledge. Just hanging there, screaming and yelling for help. Then along comes another person. Maybe it's a cowboy on a horse, or some other hero, and he hollers, "Hold on!"

Me and Summer made fun every single time we heard that. And we'd talked about it more than once, wondering if a person couldn't think of something more useful to say under those circumstances. Like, "I'm gittin' you a rope," or "I'm puttin' a horse under you." Or a mattress, or a haystack. Whatever.

But, hold on?

But now that's what I wanted to say to Summer—"Hold on!" And I knew it was useless, because just like the figure on the cliff, she already *was* holding on for dear life.

Without a word I cleaned up the floor and helped her clean herself, and then I led her back to the apartment. She stopped on the stairs, did a slow turn, and looked at me. Her face was miserable.

"What's wrong with me, Lyric?" she whispered.

"I don't know, Summer."

"Will I get better?"

"Sure you will. You're gonna get all better real soon."

"I hope so." She said it tired and slow. "It'll have to be soon, or it'll be too late."

"Too late?"

"Yeah, 'cause I think I'm disappearing, Lyric. I'm just . . . disappearing."

We went on up the stairs, and I tried not to stare at her. But I couldn't help it. Her eyes darted around constantly. They didn't usta do that. Her fingers fluttered like crippled birds. She moved slow. She was bent over. She was troubled. *She looked old.*

———

I waited up for Poppy to get home from work. I told him what had happened, and that strange thing Summer had said. He was buttering a piece of corn bread, and his knife stopped in mid-air like it forgot what to do next.

"Disappearing?" he whispered. Then he laid the knife down on the plate real gentle and his bread beside it. "Yeah, Lyric, I know that's how she feels. She told me her shadow had left her."

"She thinks she has no shadow?"

"That's what she thinks," Poppy said sadly.

I recalled it was her shadow that made her so big on the walls and ceiling that night. Now she thought it was gone.

Poppy just sat there with his hands folded up under his chin and his elbows propped on the table, staring at his plate. Seemed like his appetite had left him.

I went to bed then, and a couple of hours passed, I reckon, when I woke up to the sound of the hall window going up. I turned my head toward Summer and saw that she was sleeping soundly. The medicine did that for her.

I listened to her deep breathing for a moment. I remembered how she had once said to me, "Did you ever think what a mysterious thing sleep is? You go down deep inside yourself, you know. You go in there and you talk to another you. And together y'all figure out how you're gonna do things the next day. That's what sleeping's all about. It's time out to plan your strategy."

Well, it was for sure she needed all the strategy she could get right now, so I was careful not to disturb her as I slipped out of bed, wrapped myself up in a blanket, put on my shoes, and went into the hallway. A blast of cold air hit me in the face. The window was open, and I could see Poppy standing on the roof in his overcoat. He was taking in the peace of the night. I closed the bedroom door behind me real quiet, climbed out there, and stood beside him. He put an arm across my shoulder and smiled down at me.

The cold weather seemed to have cleared up the haze that usually lay over the city, and we just stood there together looking at the royal-blue sky with a bright bold moon shining on the snow and ice. There were a trillion stars.

"Can't sleep?" I whispered to Poppy.

"No, too much on my mind," he said.

There was ice on the roof, and if you didn't watch out, you could go sliding down over the side. So we stood in the same spot, without moving.

"Poppy, you worried 'bout Summer?"

He gave a long heavy sigh. "Yeah, a wise man once said, 'Why worry when you can pray?', but somehow I can't help it. I keep wishing your mama was here to tell me what to do."

"I don't reckon there's much you *can* do," I whispered. "Can you?"

He was silent.

"Poppy, do you think she woulda been all right if we'd stayed put back home?"

"You mean if she'd married Anderson Biddle and got

half of the A&P?" Poppy said, and looked down at me. I could tell his eyes were twinkling.

We laughed softly together.

"No, that would drive anybody crazy," I said. "But do you think moving up here made her sick?"

Poppy sighed again. "No, Lyric. I asked the doctor that same thing. And I asked him if I took her home would she be all right again, and he said no. He said there's always been this dormant seed in Summer's mind. And he said the move to Michigan might've triggered it to come alive, but if we had stayed in Virginia something else would've done the job just as good."

"A seed?" I said in a whisper. "What does that mean?"

"It means she inherited this tendency for mental illness, Lyric. It's been there all along just waitin' to hatch. I'll declare I don't know who in the world she got it from."

"Does that mean I got it, too?" I said.

"No, Lyric. The doctor says we're not to worry about you. You know in the past Summer did odd things, but not you. She's always been a little strange."

I nodded. He was right. But nobody had thought she was sick in the head. It was just how she was. We never dreamed she was harboring this seed of mental illness.

"Something was bound to trigger it, the doctor said," Poppy went on. "And adolescence is the usual age for it to go off. It's called schizophrenia."

So now the monster had a name.

We looked at the factory and the icy river shining in the

moonlight. There was an eerie hollowness in the air. Then I was almost sure that I heard a wolf howling. And its lonesomeness went echoing through the frozen streets of Flint. I shivered. I knew it was bound to be my imagination; so why did I glance up at Poppy? If he heard anything, he didn't let on. But he hugged me closer to him.

twelve

I've found us a house," Poppy said one morning at breakfast. Summer was still in bed. I think it was around the middle of February. He was grinning from ear to ear. "And it's perfect."

"What kind of house?" I said excitedly.

"Two bedrooms, living room, dining room, kitchen, and a bathroom!"

"Hallelujah! Our own bathroom!" I said.

"And a basement, too," he said.

We had never lived in a house with a basement, but it seemed like all the houses in Michigan had one. We couldn't figure out how come.

"Where's it at?" I said.

"Brand Court. It's still in the Zimmerman School district, so you won't have to change schools."

"Thank Jesus for that."

"It's a short little street out there to itself. It'll be kinda private."

"What about furniture?"

"Well, that's something else. Lucky for us, the people living there now, the Hamiltons—they're friends of Henry's—are moving back to Missouri, and they can't take all their furniture, so they're leaving some of it for us. All I gotta do is take over the payments—about fourteen bucks a month for a bedroom and living-room suite. I think I can get some twin beds real cheap for you and Summer, and a table and four chairs. And guess what? I think I'll buy us a television set!"

"Poppy!" I hollered and clapped my hands together. "A television set!"

"Yeah," Poppy said, looking real satisfied with himself as he started to eat. "We can afford it. You've been good girls, and you deserve a little something extra. I think it'll be good for Summer. It'll occupy her mind."

"I think you're right," I said happily.

And I kissed him on the cheek.

"Wonder what my daddy would think if he could come back and see how well off we're gittin' to be?" Poppy went on.

"I wonder," I said. "He wouldn't know what to think of television, would he, Poppy?"

"I reckon not. He never even heard a radio till he was a great big boy."

For a moment we sat there in silence in our private thoughts. I didn't remember Grandpa. I wondered, if he had not died in that mining accident, would Poppy have left Virginia at all? But then again, maybe Grandpa would've come with us. How nice it would be to have more kin up here in this cold, strange place.

"What about Mama?" I said. "What in the world would she think of Flint, Michigan?"

Poppy smiled and looked away at nothing.

"She was raised in a solitary place, way high on a windy mountaintop," he said. "She told me one time for once in her life she'd like to see something besides hills and sky. So I reckon she'd like it here, Lyric."

And I reckoned she would, too.

The news about the house brightened Summer up considerable. She grew more lively, and her eyes took on some of their old sparkle. She helped me make plans for the new place. Where to put this. Where to put that. What color of curtains to get. Stuff like that.

We moved on a Saturday, and Poppy was supposed to be to work by two o'clock, so we had to get up and do everything before then. Henry helped us with his pickup truck. I don't know what we would've done without Henry. He was real good to us.

After Poppy went to work, the furniture store delivered twin beds for me and Summer, a small dinette set, and the treasured television. But we couldn't watch it yet. There already was an antenna on the top of the house, but we didn't know how to use it. We would have to wait for Henry to hook it up for us.

Summer helped me make the beds, hang up our clothes, and put away things. We worked side by side, sometimes singing in harmony. It was a happy day.

Brand Court was only a few blocks from Glenwood, but

quieter, and less tacky. This was the white house we always dreamed we would live in someday, tiny but tidy, with green shutters and a wrought-iron railing around the porch. It sat at the end of the street against a knoll. There was no front yard, but a small back yard where the Hamiltons had to leave their children's swing set because they hadn't room to haul it back to Missouri.

You went to the basement from the kitchen. And that was something Summer was afraid of. I couldn't get her to go down there even to look at it. She said there were probably wolves hiding under the stairs. But I knew there was nothing but an old wringer washing machine that could still wash clothes pretty good, and shelves against the wall where we could put things we didn't use a lot. After living in two rooms, never had any place seemed so spacious!

The rent was twenty-five dollars a month, which was a bargain. We had furniture in every room, and we had little extra things like hooks in the cabinets to hang up your teacups. In our bedroom me and Summer had new wallpaper with Southern belles on it. They were strolling around under magnolia trees, and carrying tiny umbrellas that matched their dresses.

I remember how we would walk into the bathroom just to look, and to touch the sink maybe. To make sure it was real, I reckon.

We stayed up late to surprise Poppy and he was tickled when he came home from work to find two shining faces and a hot meal waiting for him on our new table. With grateful hearts we sat down and joined hands while

Poppy voiced our thanks to Jesus. Things were looking up.

That night after me and Summer climbed into our twin beds, she said to me, "This feels peculiar, Lyric. It's the first time I can remember that you and me slept in separate beds."

"Want me to come over there with you till you go to sleep?" I said.

"No," she answered after a moment. "I gotta get used to it."

We didn't say anything else. I wondered if her dreams could still get into my head now that we were sleeping apart. I hoped not. I didn't like her dreams.

We had privacy in our new place, just like Poppy had said. None of my classmates from Zimmerman lived on our street, so they wouldn't be seeing Summer and asking me about her. Funny thing about the city. You didn't know what your next-door neighbor was doing, and sometimes you didn't know their names even. Back home, everybody in the county would've known about Summer by now.

Poppy got us a telephone. He told us it didn't have any electricity in it, so Summer wasn't afraid. It was the first one we'd ever had, and I was tickled, but I didn't give anybody at school my number. I was afraid my friends might call and Summer would answer. Then I would have some explainin' to do. Sometimes I wanted to call one of them at night after Summer was in bed, but I had told them we didn't have a phone. So I would just look with yearning at the phone sittin' there silent, and think to myself someday Summer'll be all right again. Someday we'll both be talking on the phone for hours, like normal teenagers do. But for now . . .

One time Gladys said, "Lyric, that first week of school you told me you had a sister at Central High School, but ever since then, you haven't said a thing about her, and when I bring it up, you change the subject. Do you or don't you have a sister?"

We were in the lunchroom, and Yolanda and Nadine were listening. They stopped eating to look at me. They all waited for me to answer.

With my fork I moved the food around on my tray. It was something they called goulash. Hamburger meat and tomatoes in macaroni. Yankee food.

"Yeah, I got a sister," I said softly, without looking up.

"Is she still at Central?" Gladys said.

"No, she had to quit school," I said. "She's been sick."

"I'm so sorry," Nadine said sweetly. "What's wrong with her?"

I didn't know what to say then, so I didn't say anything. Instead, I stuffed my mouth full. They kept on looking at me, then at each other. Drek'ly Gladys and Nadine shrugged and went back to their own goulash. But Yolanda couldn't let a matter drop. She went on with it.

"Well, I want to know what the big mystery is," she said. "What's wrong with her?"

"None of your business!" I said hotly, and that was that. My best friends knew I had a sick sister at home, but that's all they knew. I reckoned nobody else knew anything, and that's how I wanted it.

thirteen

All through March in our snug little house at the end of our private street, me and Summer watched television every free minute. She was afraid to go near it, so I turned it on for her first thing in the morning, and it stayed on till she went to bed at night. We even took our food into the living room, and sat on the sofa and ate. She was enchanted. I guess I was, too.

Every day when I came home from school we watched *Queen for a Day*. It was real good. A bunch of women would get up there and tell their hard-luck stories, and one of them was chosen by the audience to be queen for a day. Then she would get a crown and all kinds of prizes.

We learned to repeat the regular parts right along with Jack Bailey: "Would *you* like to be queen for a day?" And Summer always added, "Yes, I would!"

We also loved *Coke Time* on Wednesday and Friday nights, which starred Eddie Fisher, and *Name That Tune* on Tuesday night. We were real good at naming the tunes.

And on Saturday nights we loved *The Jimmy Durante*

Show. We would both say, "Good night, Mrs. Callabash, wherever you are," right along with Jimmy Durante. He said that at the end of each show as he was walking away under the spotlights.

"Reckon what he means by that?" we wondered out loud. "Reckon who Mrs. Callabash is?"

Then one night Summer said, "It's me."

"You?" I said with a laugh.

"Yeah," she said dreamily. "I'm Mrs. Callabash. It's a secret code for me. Jimmy Durante is talking to me."

"I know you're kidding," I said. "Ain't you?"

"No, I'm not."

"Don't start with that stuff again, Summer," I said crossly.

"What stuff?" she said seriously. "Jimmy Durante is in love with me."

And Summer didn't seem to think that was a weird thing to say.

Another time we were watching Edgar Bergen with his dummies when Summer said, "I think somebody's throwing their voice into my head like that."

"Like what?" I said.

"Like Edgar Bergen does with his dolls, Charlie McCarthy and Mortimer Snerd. Know what I mean? It's called ventriloquism."

I knew about the voices, but she had never called it ventriloquism before.

"That's it," she said softly. "Somebody's throwing voices into my head."

"And what do they say?"

"All kinds of things. They say all kinds of things to me, and I can't make them hush."

Another show we liked was *The Perry Como Show*. One night me and Poppy were awakened around 4 a.m. by Summer singing. Her voice sounded so beautiful that night, it was downright unearthly. She was out there on the swing set in the back yard in her nightgown, just swingin' and singin' Perry Como's theme song.

> *Dream along with me*
> *I'm on my way to the stars*
> *Come along, come along*
> *Leave your worries far behind!*

We went out and got her and led her back into the house. Her skin was like ice, but she didn't seem to be cold. She went on singing. She was also laughing a real funny laugh that didn't come from her heart at all, just from her throat.

The next morning I asked her, "Why did you do such a thing?"

"They told me to do it," she replied.

"Who told you?"

"The voices."

"They told you to go outside in the cold with nothing on your arms and feet?"

"Yeah, it was the President. He has appointed me to investigate Communism."

"And that's why you were out there?"

"See, it's Mamie Eisenhower's birthday, and Jimmy Durante couldn't go," she went on.

"Summer, talk sense to me!" I said, stomping my foot in total exasperation.

"They told me to," she said lamely, then she added, "Jibble, jibble, groggle . . ."

"Groggle" was a new word she had invented. It made perfect sense to her.

That day Poppy called the doctor, and he upped the dosage of Summer's medication.

"Doctor says the day is coming when pills won't control her behavior," Poppy whispered to me. "Her body develops a tolerance to them, see? And after a while they'll have no effect on her."

"What will we do then, Poppy?"

"I don't know. I just don't know. Doctor says we might have to commit her."

"Commit her to what?"

"To the asylum in Pony-ac, Lyric," he said sadly.

He meant Pontiac. Everybody back home said *Pony-ac*, but it was one of those words I had learned to say right at school.

"Oh, no, Poppy, not a lunatic asylum!"

"Listen, Lyric, even with my good insurance from GM, the medical bills are awful. I can't begin to pay for all the treatment she needs. I can't even pronounce or halfway understand all the things they want to do for her. But Doctor says if I put her in Pony-ac, I can make her a ward of the State of Michigan, and they'll take care of her. They'll know what to do for her. They can give her the very best of care for free."

"If she's made a ward of the state, will they ever give her back to us?" I said.

"I reckon so, when she gets better," Poppy said, "they'll give her back. Yeah, they'll give her back."

"But will she get better?"

"I just don't know," Poppy said wearily. "The only thing I know for sure is that she needs a lot more help than she's gettin' now."

"But in the asylum she won't have us, Poppy," I said. "Summer has never been away from us."

"I know," Poppy said. "We won't do anything a'tall yet, Lyric. We'll take it one day at a time."

He paused and repeated, "We'll take it one day at a time."

fourteen

M y fourteenth birthday fell on the last Saturday in March that year. It seemed funny to look outside and see traces of snow. And the ground was still half-frozen. Back home in Virginia the crocuses would be pushing up through the soft black dirt, and the buttercups would be in bloom.

But back home I wouldn't be studying music in school. Yolanda, Nadine, and Gladys wouldn't be there either. Poppy wouldn't be able to afford a television and a telephone. And he couldn't give me ten dollars and tell me to go shopping for my birthday, which is what he did!

"Ten whole dollars?" I said. "You mean it, Poppy?"

"Sure I mean it. You didn't have much of a Christmas. Buy yourself something pretty."

Summer heard that, and I was surprised when she said she wanted to go shopping with me.

So I told her, "Summer, I want you to go with me, but you have to promise not to act up."

"I won't," she said weakly.

"We can spend the whole day down on Saginaw Street like we did when we first came to Flint, 'member?"

"Yeah," she said, smiling. "Can we buy something good to eat?"

"Sure."

At school I'd been hearing about this place downtown called Kewpie's where they sold hamburgers and hot dogs, and they said if you wanted to meet cute boys, Kewpie's was the place to go. But I was afraid we might run into somebody I knew there.

Then I realized I was doing it again. I was trying to hide Summer, and I couldn't do that forever. Besides, she had seemed better since the doctor increased her medication, so I decided to take a chance and tell her about Kewpie's.

"Goody! I'd like to meet me some cute boys," she said with a giggle. "Let's eat lunch there."

We dressed up in our black slacks which everybody called slim-jims that year, and oversized white shirts, and we decided not to wear boots. It was warm enough to wear our penny loafers and bobby socks. Boots didn't look good with slim-jims.

I helped Summer cut and clean her fingernails, and polish them. Her hands looked very nice then, and her hair had grown out to its usual length. We tucked it back behind her ears, and clipped it there with silver hair bows.

Then we both put on our light jackets instead of overcoats, and headed out to the bus stop, as giddy as we'd been the week of the Centennial. That seemed like a long time ago.

At Kresge's I picked out some Precious Pink lipstick to match the nail polish we were both wearing, which I had bought Summer for her birthday. I got some other stuff too, and when I realized half of my money was spent, we left the dime store before it all disappeared, and went window shopping.

Though the air was chilly, the sun was shining bright, and the sky was perfectly blue, about the color of Summer's eyes, so I told her that. She smiled and hooked her arm through mine.

"Your eyes are that blue, too!" she said. "You are lookin' so grownup these days, Lyric, and so cute."

"Ree . . . al . . . lee?"

To get a compliment from Summer was special, because I knew she was always honest with me. I could trust her opinion.

"Yeah," she said. "You're real pretty."

I wisht then I could say the same thing about her. But the madness and medication had taken its toll on her appearance.

Before I could think of something nice to say, Summer said, "My looks don't matter to me anymore."

It was like she had read my mind. "When a person is like me, your worries are more important than anything else. I usta get all tangled up in my mind. But lately I've been thinking clear, and I've been given sacred visions. I see all the millions—I reckon even billions—of people who lived on this earth before us, and . . ."

"Don't start, Summer," I pleaded.

"No, I'm serious now," she said and began to talk real fast. She was trying to get everything out before her train of thought derailed. That was apt to happen to her sometimes.

"A hundred years ago there was a girl who was as troubled as me . . . and the world revolved around her worries, at least in her mind it did . . . but today she lays buried in a grave . . . and nobody knows what happened to her . . . or remembers her name or anything about her . . . she's forgotten, Lyric . . . *forgotten* . . . and the world goes on without her, on and on, turning around and around . . . and other girls have walked the earth . . . boys, too . . . millions of 'em . . . each one growing up laughing and dancing and having sweethearts . . . and thinking they're the only one who ever felt this way . . . the only one who ever had troubles . . . then they are lost and forgotten . . ."

"What makes you think of things like that?" I said.

"I don't know. I just think. I think all the time. And voices come to me and tell me things. A hundred years from now—in the year 2056—I'll be in a grave, and another girl will be wondering . . ."

Summer stopped abruptly to look at some books that were on display in the window of a bookstore. There was one on ghosts. Summer pointed to it and said, "That's what ghosts are, you know. They are people like me from long ago. And they're still wandering the earth, all caught up in their earthly problems and they can't give it up."

"Summer, you said you wouldn't do this."

"I know," she said, and we continued walking down the street. "I just wisht I knew how to keep from fading away."

"Try not to think about it."

But there was no shutting her up.

"Out of all those millions, only a handful are remembered," she went on sadly. "Sometimes in books they are kept alive."

We walked along in silence for a minute.

Then, "Will you write a book about me, Lyric?"

"Sure I will. Now hush up!" She was getting on my nerves.

"Promise?"

"I promise!" I said irritably. "Let's go eat lunch."

So we went to Kewpie's. Lots of other teenagers were there, but nobody I knew. I was relieved. There were three cute boys in the next booth, and they smiled at us.

After a while one of the boys said, "Hey, you," and we turned around to talk to him.

"What's your name?"

"Lyric," I said.

"Summer," she said.

"Where do you go to school?"

"Zimmerman," I said, and Summer didn't say anything.

"Oh, I know some kids from Zimmerman. Do you know . . . ?"

He started naming people, and some of them I knew and some of them I didn't. We got to talking, and the other two boys joined in. They said their names were Larry, Curly, and Moe, but I knew better. I said they just *acted* like Larry, Curly, and Moe. Then they laughed and gave me their real names—Steve, Michael, and Mark, Michigan names.

"We met each other through the busy line," Steve said.

"The what?"

"Don't you know about the busy line?" Mark said.

"No, what is it?"

"It's a telephone number you can dial," Mark explained. "And you always get a busy signal—always. But if you listen hard, over the signal you can hear other kids yelling."

"Yelling?" I said.

"Yeah, they'll be yelling their telephone numbers," Michael joined in.

I smiled at him. He was the cutest one. He was my pick.

"And you can hear the numbers over the busy signal?" I said.

I didn't know much about telephones, but that seemed peculiar to me. How could it be?

"Yeah," Michael went on. "I don't know how it happens, but you can hear."

"So everybody yells their phone numbers into this line," Steve went on, "and if you listen, you can zero in on a particular voice. So you call the number the voice is yelling, and that's how lots of kids get to know each other."

"That's right—through the busy line," Michael finished. "And here's the number. Try it."

He handed me a little piece of napkin with a phone number on it.

It was then I realized that nobody was talking to Summer. The boys were saying all this stuff to me. They were ignoring her, and she had gone quiet. I was trying to figure out how to draw her into the conversation when she excused herself to go to the rest room.

I went right on talking and joking with the boys until Summer got back. Then I saw that she had taken my Precious Pink lipstick and tried to put it on her lips, but she had missed. It was all over the place, up above and below her mouth, but she seemed to be real pleased with herself. She was grinning this big grin, and I could see she had lipstick on her teeth, too. She looked absolutely grotesque.

And for one awful second I saw the face of crazy Sadie where my sister's face shoulda been.

"Look what you've done," I said to her with an embarrassed laugh, "you've smeared your lipstick."

The boys got quiet as they stared at her, and I felt my face turn red. All the other kids there were sniggering and pointing at her.

"Go back in there and fix it," I whispered to her.

She stopped grinning and, without a word, got up and returned to the rest room. I didn't feel like talking and joking around anymore, so I said nothing else to the boys. I didn't even look up as I took money out of my purse and started to the cash register to pay.

"What's wrong with your mom?" Mark said to me as I went by the boys' table.

"My mom?" I stopped in my tracks and faced him just in time to see Michael elbow him in the ribs.

"Yeah, ain't that woman your mom?"

I didn't answer him. I went on my way and paid the cashier; then I stood by the door to wait for Summer to come out of the rest room. I felt so bad I wanted to go on home and forget about spending the rest of my birthday money.

After a while Michael came to me and said, "Hey, if you're waiting for that woman, she went out the other door."

"What!"

"Yeah, she went out that side door while you were paying."

I hurried out the door he pointed to and looked up and down the street, but Summer was nowhere to be seen. Then I went back inside and double-checked the rest room. No Summer. I ran through Kewpie's to the outside again. All the kids were watching me now, but I was hardly aware of them. This was no time to be embarrassed. I was scared.

Breathlessly, I went back in and said to Michael, "Did you see which way she went?"

"No, I just saw her go out the door," he said. "Sorry. What's wrong with her?"

"She's sick," I said. I was practically wringing my hands. "She shouldn't be alone."

"I'll help you look for her," he said kindly as he climbed out of the booth.

Together me and Michael walked up and down the street real fast, looking everywhere. No luck. Then we walked slowly back to Kewpie's.

There was nothing left but to call Poppy at work. I had never had to do that before, but his number was in my purse. He had given it to me for emergencies, and I reckoned this was one. There was a phone booth on the street corner.

"Stay right where you are!" Poppy said to me. "I'll be there soon's I can get away."

I hung up, turned to Michael, and said, "Thanks for your help. There's nothing else you can do."

"You sure?" he said. Later I remembered how good-hearted he had been.

"I'm sure. You can go on back to your friends."

At least I think that's what I said. My thoughts were racing. What to do? What to do? Oh, Summer, why did you do this? Were your feelings hurt to be left out? Or didn't you know what you were doing? Where is your poor little mind taking you to?

I sat on a bench at the bus stop in front of the restaurant, waiting for Poppy. Pretty soon Michael, Mark, and Steve came out the door and saw me. They all stopped to tell me goodbye, and said they hoped Summer would be all right.

I said something to them. I don't know what.

"Be sure to call the busy line when you get a chance," Michael said. "I think you'll find it interesting."

"Yeah, thanks," I mumbled.

fifteen

Poppy got there on a bus in about half an hour, and we started walking up and down the street together, asking people in the business places if they had seen Summer. We described her as best we could, knowing that once a person saw that haunted face, they were not likely to forget it. But nobody could recall seeing her.

"At that bus stop," Poppy said to me. "Do you think she might've caught a bus?"

"I don't know if she had any money with her. Do you know?"

"No," Poppy said. "She ain't asked me for money in a long time. She never went anywheres."

Then he let out one of those long, heavy sighs. "I think there's nothing left to do but call the police."

I reckoned he was right. So we called the police, and they came, and they went through a long list of questions for us. They asked for a picture, and Poppy had one in his billfold, but it was of that beautiful Summer in our memories who didn't much resemble the sick Summer. I knew that's why Poppy had not shown it to the people in the business places.

Poppy told the policemen how bad off she was, and they could see how worried we were. They patted Poppy on the back and me on the head and told us to go on home now and try not to worry. They would call us in a while.

So we did go home, and all through the rest of the afternoon we paced the floor. Ever' now and then we peered out the window. We sat down at the eating table once or twice and nibbled on some leftovers. We watched the phone and willed it to ring. But we never talked about Summer, or about anything else. We had run out of things to say. Still, I knew all the while Poppy's mind was going a hundred miles an hour, like mine was . . . wondering, worrying . . .

She didn't have on her boots, and it was getting colder outside as the day fell into evening. She didn't have on her winter coat either.

What could she be thinking? Did she remember what Poppy had said that time about bad things happening to young girls in big cities? Did she remember our telephone number? Did she know how to call from a public phone? She must be so scared!

I didn't know how many practical things she remembered. Did she even know her address? Why, oh why didn't we go over these things with her?

Ring, phone, ring . . .

I recalled another spring day back in the hills when me and Summer went to visit Aunt June without Poppy's permission. We were only six and nine then, I think. And we had walked all by ourselves down to the highway, playing and picking violets along the way, while Poppy was worried sick. Now I knew how he had felt.

We heard a car door slam and hurried to the window. There was a man opening the passenger door of a Buick, and someone was getting out. The man was Bill from Glenwood Avenue, and the someone was Summer!

We rushed outside. I went to Summer, and Poppy grabbed Bill up off of the ground by his collar and pushed him against the car real rough. I thought he was bound to kill the poor man.

"What were you doing with my girl!" he hollered right in Bill's face.

Bill turned red, and his eyes looked like they were gonna pop out of his head.

"What's the matter with Poppy?" Summer whispered frantically to me.

"Whadda *you* think?" I snapped. "He was worried to death!"

"Did you hurt her?" Poppy said to Bill through clenched teeth.

"I sw . . . swear to God, Mr. C . . . Compton," Bill stammered. "I ain't t . . . touched her. She come to Glenwood. She said she walked from downtown. And she ast me to take her to a pi'ture show. But I wouldn't do it. I talked her into coming home. And I brung her here. I swear to God that's all there was to it. I swear."

Poppy seemed unsure of what to do next. Slowly he let

go of Bill. Summer started humming to herself and looking up at the sky, like she saw a vision up there. It was another of those peculiar things she used to do as a little girl when she didn't want to see what was happening in the real world. But I hadn't seen her do it in a long time.

"I know she's mental," Bill said real low, but I still heard him. Then he rubbed his neck where Poppy had grabbed him. "I wouldn't hurt her, Mr. Compton."

"All right," Poppy mumbled. "All right."

Then he took Summer by the arm and hauled her into the house. He was upset. He didn't know how to act.

Me and Bill were left standing there looking at each other.

"Thanks," I mumbled, "for bringing her home."

He straightened himself up, and said crossly, "She's been calling me a lot."

"She don't know what she's doin'," I said. "She's sick."

"Well, can you git her to stop?"

"I'll try."

And with that Bill got back in his car and drove away real quick. I went into the house. Summer had gone to our room while Poppy was on the phone with the police. When I went in there, she was sitting on the edge of the bed, still humming, and smiling a silly smile.

I sat down beside her on the bed. "Summer, why did you run away from me like that?"

"Bill's in love with me," she said.

Then I lost it. "Why are you acting so ugly? He said

you've been calling him, and he wants you to stop! Why don't you straighten up? Do you want to go to the asylum? Do you?"

"What do you mean, Lyric?" she said in a hoarse whisper.

"Nothing."

"What did you mean by that?"

I could feel her trembling, and her hands started fluttering.

"I didn't mean anything," I said. "I was foolin'."

"Is Poppy gonna put me in a *place*?"

"'Course not!"

But she knew I was lying to her. I had lost my temper and what good had it done? Now she had something else to be afraid of.

Then, just like that, I saw Summer's face go totally blank. It was uncanny and unnatural. That's what it was. And I could tell by her lack of expression that nobody was home in there. Summer had retreated to a safe place deep inside where nothing or nobody could touch her.

"Try to get her to take a bath, why don'cha, Lyric?" Poppy said to me as he was going out the door to work the next Saturday.

For the entire week Summer had not reappeared. Only her body was there and it would not bathe or dress or comb its hair. It stunk, and it stayed in bed most all the time, staring at the ceiling.

"I'll try, Poppy."

But when I suggested a bath, Summer said in her tiny voice, "I can't. Water washes me away."

"No, no, Summer," I said. "That's silly. Water does not wash you away."

Finally, I managed to coax her into the bathroom by telling her that Poppy wanted his little girls to be squeaky clean. That took us both back to our childhood in Glory Bottom when we were waiting for Poppy to come home from the mines and spend some time with us.

"Sometimes I miss the hills," she said softly, and I knew her wandering mind had returned, but I didn't know for how long.

I helped her ease into the tub of hot, soapy water, and I washed her hair. Then I sat on the john and talked to her while she relaxed in the suds.

"Would you like to go back home?" I asked her.

"No!" she came back in a flash. "If you look at the world as a house, Lyric, Glory Bottom is the crawl space."

I laughed a genuine laugh then. Yeah, I reckoned the real Summer had made a brief visit. Always the clever one. And she smiled a genuine smile.

Later I helped her dry and wrap herself up in a robe. As she wiped the steam away from the mirror over the sink I came up behind her and our eyes met in the reflection.

"See, Lyric? I'm fading away," she said softly. "See? I'm almost gone."

sixteen

there were things about living in the hills that I didn't miss a bit. Like kids coming to school with lice, or smelling like pee. Wormy kids. Kids with crusty elbows and knees 'cause they had no soap or running water in their houses. Things like the stink of the slate dumps. Coal trucks lumbering over the dirt roads, trailing black dust to coat everything in their wake. Outhouses and shacks hanging off the hillsides.

You didn't see things like that in the city of Flint. But you didn't see spring coming to life either, at least not the way I remembered it. Take the emerald green of the hills. So brilliant it hurt your eyes.

But maybe it wasn't that radiant at all, I thought. Maybe I dreamed it. Lots of times, things are not really as good as you remember them later. On the other hand, some stuff has a tendency to fade, like the faces of my kinfolks. We had been gone only seven months, and I found them hard to recollect. And what about my former classmates? I had forgotten some of their names!

This is how we let things slip away, I told myself. We get all involved in other things, allowing the present to fade into the past.

> *. . . summer turns to winter*
> *and the present disappears.*

In my new life I was falling in love with Gilbert and Sullivan's *The Mikado*, which the combined music classes at Zimmerman were fixin' to produce. You wouldn't never find something like this back home. And you wouldn't find wonderful music teachers like Mrs. Gaspar and Mr. German either.

We did a lot of singing in Mrs. Gaspar's music class, and my friends were always saying, "Wow, Lyric, you're really good!" It made me proud. I only wisht they could hear me and Summer harmonize together, but I didn't mention it.

They told me I had a chance for a part in *The Mikado*, not just in the chorus, but a good part like Pitti-Sing or Peep-Bo. I didn't dare hope for Yum-Yum. Everybody said Yum-Yum would be a ninth-grader. I was so excited I learned all the lyrics to all the songs. I went around humming "Three Little Maids from School Are We," until Poppy started humming it, too. He laughed when I told him what he was singing.

"Tell me about this play," he said to me. "Will I get to see it?"

"Sure, if you want to," I said, but already I was wondering what we would do with Summer while Poppy came to the play. To take her along was out of the question. She had started making funny whistling noises, and she couldn't keep her mind on anything, not even her favorite television shows anymore. Sometimes she'd jump up and start pacing and jabbering right in the middle of one. I could imagine her doing that during *The Mikado*.

It was three weeks into April when I had to stay after school for the tryouts. By then it didn't get dark so early, and I wasn't worried about getting home to Summer. I told her I was going to try out for a part in an operetta and I would be late coming home, but she wasn't listening. At least I thought she wasn't. She was sitting there on the edge of her bed, rocking and shaking her leg. Her doctor called what she was doing perseverating. He said it was a common thing for a mentally ill person to do. She was also making that funny noise.

"I'll be ri'cheer with her till two o'clock," Poppy reassured me. "I'll give her something t'eat before I go to work, and she'll be O.K. till you come home."

Nearabout half of the kids at Zimmerman showed up in the auditorium for the tryouts after school. Mr. German and Mrs. Gaspar were sitting at the piano deciding how they were gonna do stuff, while everybody else was milling around, talking and making noise. So I went off into a corner by myself and started going over Pitti-Sing's part.

I was mouthing the words low to myself when I became aware that something was going on about halfway back in the auditorium. I didn't want to be distracted right then, so I closed my eyes and concentrated harder.

Then a hush fell, and I heard a familiar, "Jibble . . . jibble . . ."

Lordy mercy, don't let that mean what I think it means!

Slowly I turned my head to where my classmates had congregated. I could see only the backs of young people crowded around something, but I *knew* what was at the center of their attention. I walked over there and eased myself far enough amongst them that I could see.

Summer was sitting there at the end of one of the rows of seats shaking her leg furiously and making that funny blowing sound with her mouth. She was real agitated. Her eyes were darting rapidly from place to place, settling on nothing.

I realized in that moment what Yolanda had meant when she had said, "They'll peck you to death if you're different."

Peck! Peck!

"Look at that funny woman!"

"Jibble, jibble," Summer said, and my classmates burst into laughter.

Peck! Peck!

"Hey, crater face!"

Peck! Peck!

"Where's your shoes at, looney?"

"Groggle."

"Did you say, 'Gobble, gobble?' "

More laughter.

My darkest emotions surfaced.

First shame.

There was simply no keeping this skeleton in the closet. It was obvious she *had* heard me that morning, and she had come to see the tryouts.

Then anger.

How come she could understand only what she wanted to understand? How come she pretended she wasn't listening to me? Why was she playing games with me?

And grief.

Oh, Mama, Mama, I miss you so! Why did you have to die and leave me all alone like this?

Of all the things that might have come into my mind right then, why did I think of that? Why should I suddenly long for my mother with all my heart and soul when I had never felt that way before?

Then a jumbled collage of the past and present played out before me like one of Summer's ghostly hallucinations.

I see that she is wearing her house slippers . . . and I remember Summer teaching me how to tie my shoe strings.

I hear her making that sound with her mouth . . . and I remember Summer teaching me to whistle.

Her dress is on backwards . . . and I remember Summer washing a stain out of my favorite dress on a Saturday night so I can wear it to Sunday School the next morning.

Her hair needs combing . . . and I remember Summer gently brushing the tangles out of my baby-fine hair.

A thousand acts of love . . . saving her singing money to buy me a present . . . kissing away my tears . . .

"Gobble, gobble!" Dewey the heckler mocks her . . . and I remember Summer rescuing me from bullies at school.

I pushed my way through the kids and gave Dewey a shove that sent him sprawling into the crowd. He yelped. Somebody caught him and kept him on his feet.

I went to my sister's side. "It's O.K., Summer," I said. "I'm here."

She jumped out of her seat, grabbed my arm, and clung to it. Everybody got quiet then. They were all staring with their mouths open. They were wondering if Lyric Compton knew this funny-lookin' person. Maybe they were wondering if we were kin. And they couldn't wait to find out!

"Jibble, jibble, groggle . . ." Summer said. She wanted to tell me something, but the right words were lost to her.

Whisperings rippled through the group like a breeze through leaves. I saw my three best friends standing there together gaping.

"This is my sister, Summer," I said directly to Yolanda, Nadine, and Gladys.

I said it clearly and dramatically, just as I had rehearsed saying, "I am Pitti-Sing, sister to Yum-Yum."

Some kids sniggered, but my friends looked upon us kindly.

At that moment Summer tugged at my sleeve excitedly and said, "Lyric, am I queen for a day?"

Then she covered her face with her hands as the auditorium exploded with laughter. You couldn't much blame them, I thought. Maybe it was kinda funny. But it didn't feel funny to me. I was afraid that I might cry. I could feel the hot angry tears just ready to boil over, but I wouldn't let them.

"What's going on?" I heard as Mrs. Gaspar and Mr. German stepped into the circle and saw me there with Summer.

"My sister's sick," I said quietly. "I'll be taking her home now."

On the way home Summer said to me, "I didn't know where you were at, Lyric, and I needed you. There was a goblin. He was 'lectric . . . a little 'lectric goblin, and I was afraid of him . . . the F.B.I. sent him to spy on me."

I was thinking that night that it was getting harder and harder to love Summer, and to forgive her for her weirdness. When I discovered that thought in my head, I felt so guilty I went into the bedroom where she was supposed to be sleeping to check on her and give her a hug.

There she was sitting in the middle of the bed playing with matches. She was striking one after another and throwing them, lit, onto the floor, where they burnt little brown spots into the linoleum.

I had to fight Summer to get the matches away from her, but I finally did it, and I hid all the others that I could find in the house. The next day she lit a candle from the flame on the gas stove. Poppy found out when he saw that the stove was on, and when he went in to ask Summer about it, she was burning a candle right beside her curtains.

So now we had something else to be afraid of. We couldn't let her out of our sight.

seventeen

On a Friday evening in May I went to see *The Mikado* by myself. I mouthed all the words as they were sung onstage, and my heart hurt because I felt so left out.

It was Poppy's night off, so he stayed home with Summer. He had coaxed it out of me what had happened at the tryouts, and I could see the sadness in his eyes. In fact, he felt so bad he said he was going to hire somebody to look after Summer whenever I wanted some time to go do things like that by myself and he had to work.

"I don't want you to be embarrassed, and to be left out of things on account of her," he told me. " 'Cause then you'll start resenting your sister, and I won't let that happen."

But I didn't want to blame anything on Summer. I knew she couldn't help it. She was my sister, for crying out loud! She just couldn't help how she was. Still, it would be nice not to have to worry about her when I had something to do.

So Poppy started looking for somebody suitable to come

in for a few hours once in a while. And he found Beatrice, who was the daughter of a West Virginia feller Poppy worked with.

Bea, as everybody called her, was eighteen and done with school. She had been in Flint for two years, so her accent was mongrel. She had a boyfriend by the name of Roy Rivers, who had adopted a lot of Bea's expressions and ways because he thought they were cute, but I had learned to recognize the real thoroughbred Yankees, no matter how they acted. They always gave themselves away in little ways, like the so-called country singer on television who called a fiddle a violin.

Bea and Roy came over one Sunday evening to meet Summer, but she was sullen with them and wouldn't raise her eyes to meet theirs. She went on watching the television and wouldn't let me turn it off. Still, Bea talked to her in loud, careful words, like Summer was hard of hearing.

"Summer," Bea said, laying one hand on her arm. *"Roy and I would love to visit with you once in a while. Is that all right with you?"*

At which Summer irritably shook off Bea's hand, and didn't even answer.

"Well, that's O.K.," Bea whispered to me and Poppy. "When it comes to making friends, me and Roy never met a nut we couldn't crack, did we, Roy?"

And she turned to Roy and punched him playfully with her elbow. They both giggled. They were always giggling. But I didn't think that was so funny.

I figure about that time it dawned on Bea what she had said, 'cause she turned red.

She tried to explain, "I didn't mean anything. I meant me and Roy never met a stranger. We're just so full of ourselves, people get tickled at us all the time."

"Right!" Roy said. "That Bea's crazy as they come."

That Roy shoulda kept his mouth shut. Now they were both blushing.

Poppy explained as best he could what Summer's sickness was like, how she was liable to hurt herself or set the house on fire, and what they would be expected to do when they stayed with her, mainly just watch her close.

"We can handle that," Bea and Roy both said, and giggled again.

"It was very nice to meet you, Summer," Bea said carefully as she was leaving, but Summer ignored her.

When they were gone, me and Poppy looked at each other, wondering if we could really trust that silly couple with our Summer. But we reckoned we'd give them a chance.

When school let out at the end of May, I called the number of the busy line which Michael had given me that day at Kewpie's. Funny thing, it wasn't busy. In fact, it was Michael who answered!

"You were foolin' me!" I said with a laugh. "There's no such thing as the busy line!"

"Yeah, there really is," Michael said. "That was the

truth, and I'll give you the real number if you'd like it. But I wanted you to call me."

And that was the beginning of my friendship with Michael Beaver. We talked on the phone a lot, and Poppy let us meet for lunch at Kewpie's of a Saturday, and he would let Michael come to the house when he was there too, but he wouldn't let me go on a date yet.

With me out of school, we found that we didn't have to call on Bea to come sit with Summer. I could do lots of things I wanted to do before Poppy went to work at 2 p.m., and he was off two nights a week to look after her. But on the nights he had to work, I stayed home.

Sometimes I had a chance to go picnicking, swimming, roller skating, bowling, or to ball games and movies with my friends. There were lots of things to do in Michigan, and I took advantage of them when Poppy was at home with Summer.

Gayle Stiltner introduced us to her church, and we liked it. Lots of Southern people went there, and we started going every Sunday. Poppy went to the 9 a.m. service and I went at eleven.

About that time I discovered a sneaky streak in that mixed-up mind of Summer's. For example, she'd pretend to be just sitting and staring out the window until she thought you were not paying her any attention. Then she would very quietly go rummaging around for something to stick in the flames on the gas stove.

When I figured out what she was doing, she would run

out the door and down the street. Then I had to go chasing after her, and yelling for her through the neighborhood. She would go into people's yards and hide in the bushes or around behind the garages. When I gave up on finding her and went back home, there she was, messing around with fire again! It like to scared me witless. I caught on to that trick after the second time, luckily before she burnt the house down.

Then she took up another dangerous thing—playing with sharp things. One day I found her cutting her fingernails with a razor blade, and blood was dripping all over her housecoat. I was horrified. It made me hurt just to look at her poor hands.

That doubled our worries 'cause now we had to keep anything sharp out of her reach, and matches, too. She was still afraid to go down into the basement, so I could hide stuff from her there. Poppy took to carrying his razor blades to work with him so I wouldn't have to worry about them.

But when she wasn't mutilating herself or playing with fire, Summer was sitting quiet and doing nothing. It was easy enough to forget that she could be dangerous.

Poppy bought a picnic table for the back yard so we could eat out there in warm weather. It was a Michigan thing to do, and lots of fun. One weekend when he was off, he invited Gayle, her son, Paul, and Paul's girlfriend, Lily, over for hamburgers. He also invited Henry and his new girlfriend, Wilma Dean.

The next time, he let me invite Michael, Gladys, Nadine, Yolanda, and Yolanda's friend, Ike. That lil' ole house had never heard so much laughter! We ate out in our private back yard, and just had the best time.

I thought of how I had dreaded for other people to see Summer, because I was ashamed. But now I learned that the most important people—at least to me and Poppy— were kind. In fact, I had greatly underestimated my friends.

We all went out of our way to include Summer in our picnics, but she did not like having other people around her. In fact, she hated it, and she angrily retreated to our bedroom and slammed the door. And if me or Poppy took her something to eat and begged her to come out, she would just shout at us to go away.

"Give her time to get used to you," Poppy would say to our guests. "She'll get over it."

But she never did.

At these times when we had company, the hardest part was making Summer clean herself up before they got there. First I would go into the bathroom, run the water, and get everything ready. Then Poppy would grab Summer and force her into the bathroom. Once he had in her there, he would stand outside the door and wouldn't let her out until she had bathed, washed her hair, and put on clean clothes. And I was in there with her to make sure she did it. Oh, it made her so mad! She would cuss and cry and holler the whole time. But she would finally do what she was told, just to get out of the bathroom.

Wildflowers managed to find a place to grow out on that little knoll behind our house. One time when I looked out there I was reminded again of home. How the katydids would be doing their summer songs. How the creeks and the river would be sparkling in the afternoon sunshine. The smell of summer rain. The sky a channel of blue you had to look straight up to see. The children roaming the hills, climbing trees. Bluebells and wild pink roses. Swimming holes. Ball games in the road.

But now those images appeared in my head like a movie I had once seen that had nothing to do with me. How strange, I thought, my far home is now like a place I've only seen pictures of.

But most of the time I was too busy to remember even the pictures. I had a new home, a new life, far removed from Glory Bottom. By the time the changeover came at General Motors, we had forgotten our plans to go back to the hills for a visit. Our new life had usurped the old one.

eighteen

One Saturday in the middle of July I was invited to go with Gladys and her daddy, her brother and her brother's friend to Detroit and see the Detroit Tigers play baseball. We would be gone all day. Poppy had to work, but he said this was a chance I must not throw away, so he called Bea to come stay with Summer.

And that was the day that Summer managed to sneak matches out of one of Poppy's shirt pockets. Only it wasn't the curtains or the house she wanted to burn that day—it was herself.

"We missed her for a few minutes," Bea told me later, "and when we went into the bedroom to find her, there she was sitting in the middle of the bed holding a flaming match to her arm. It was burning the flesh of her arm at one end and her fingers at the other end. And she didn't even say 'ouch!' "

Bea had gone into a screaming fit while Roy took the matches away from Summer. She had five big ugly burned places on her left arm. Roy called Poppy at work, and he came home and took Summer to the emergency room, where they put her in the psychiatric ward again.

A new young intern cared for her this time. His name was Dr. Elliott, and he took a special interest in Summer's case.

"This child needs to be in the hospital at Pontiac," he told Poppy.

"I don't want to just lock her up," Poppy said.

"It's not a prison," the doctor said kindly. "You can take her home for holidays and vacations. And if she gets well, they'll release her. It's important for schizophrenics to know that the family still cares about them, but Summer needs medications and special treatments that you can't give her at home."

"Well, I reckon I'll consider it when school starts again," Poppy told the young doctor.

"School?" Dr. Elliott said, not understanding.

"Yeah, my other girl, Lyric, she's fourteen, and she does a real good job with Summer, but she'll be going into the ninth grade in September, and . . ."

"A fourteen-year-old girl is not capable . . . She should not even be left alone with Summer," Dr. Elliott said firmly.

Which gave Poppy something else to worry about.

"Dr. Elliott thinks taking care of Summer is too hard on you, Lyric, and too dangerous for both of you," he said to me that night. "And he could be right. Maybe it's time to, you know . . ."

"Poppy, no!" I said. "We can't just throw her out—*throw her to the wolves!*"

"I don't know what else to do, Lyric," he said. "I'll declare I don't."

"Let's try another sitter, maybe an older person this time," I suggested. "There must be somebody we can trust to stay with her just that short period, from the time you go to work until I get home from school, and maybe some evenings, too, when I have to go somewhere."

"All right," Poppy agreed. "We'll give it another shot."

When Summer returned from the hospital, she was all drugged up again, but this time the medication wore off real fast and she came out of it mad at the world.

We hired a woman named Susie to come stay with Summer for one evening. I went over to Nadine's house for a couple of hours just to see how Susie and Summer would get along. But Summer sneaked away, and we had to call the police again. She wasn't found until the next morning, when a neighbor spotted her asleep behind a bush in her yard.

Then came Margie. Summer hit her and broke her glasses. Lucy followed, and Summer cussed her out. Myrtle was locked out of the house, and Ginger was burned while trying to put out a fire . . .

One balmy afternoon in August, Poppy was at work and Summer was asleep when I first became aware of this eerie stillness in the air. I walked out on our tiny back porch to see if I could figure out what was amiss. I found myself looking up into a gray cover that reminded me of the troubled sky in the wolf nightmare—dark, turbulent, rolling.

The telephone rang, and I ran back inside to answer the ring before it woke Summer up. It was Poppy.

"Lyric," he said. "You got the television on?"

"No," I said. "Why?"

"Well, turn it on. I hear they got tornado warnings. I don't believe y'all are in the danger zone, but just the same, you watch and listen."

"Tornado warnings?" I said. "Ree . . . al . . . lee?" I thought that was exciting news, something to write home about.

"Yeah, if there comes a tornado, you follow instructions, you heah me? You do what they tell you on the television."

I turned on the TV just as a man was saying that a close tornado sounds like a train is coming into the house, and if you should happen to hear that noise, you better get yourself down in the basement fast. And that's when I figured out why Michigan houses have basements.

I heard Summer get up and go to the refrigerator. I could smell her before she entered the living room. She was drinking Kool-Aid from a coffee cup, and she looked awful. Her face was puffy from sleep, her hair filthy, and she was wearing the same shorty pajamas she had been wearing for the last four or five days. I had tried to get them off of her once, but she had fought me away.

"I'll change clothes when I get damn good and ready!" she had said hotly. "So mind your own beeswax!"

That's how she was now. Sometimes she even called me

nasty names. I mean *real* nasty. She said words that Poppy used to spank us both for saying. But nowadays he would look the other way with sad, lost eyes. He didn't know what to do.

"I wanna see Art Linkletter," Summer said.

"He's not on," I said. "There's tornado warnings. Poppy said for us to watch."

"Where's Art Linkletter?" She raised her voice.

"He's not on!" I snapped and turned up the volume so I could hear what the weatherman was saying.

"He's always on at this time!" Summer screamed. "Who's that man yonder?"

"He's talking about tornadoes," I said. "We have to listen to him."

"No! He's ugly!" she screamed again. "I hate him!"

"A tornado has been sighted on Dort Highway!" the announcer said in an urgent voice.

That was across town from us.

"I repeat . . ."

"Turn him off!" Summer bellowed at me.

"No, Summer. Listen, listen . . ."

"If you are in the Dort Highway vicinity . . ."

"If you don't turn him off . . ." Summer hissed, and suddenly lunged at me.

Before I could react, she had smashed me over the head with the coffee cup. I was stunned with the blow. The cup shattered and the pieces went flying all over the room.

I touched my head gently and felt a stickiness in my hair.

At first I thought it was only Kool-Aid, but when I looked at my fingers they were covered with blood. I wobbled in my tracks. Summer just stood there glaring at me.

I wanted to throw up.

"And another tornado has been spotted on Corunna Road!" the announcer was saying.

That was closer to us. I can't be sick right now, I thought. And I can't think of my busted head. I'll have to worry about that later.

"We've got to get down into the basement," I said to Summer.

"No, there are wolves down there!" she screamed.

"Then do as you please!" I yelled back at her. "I'm goin' where it's safe!"

And I walked unsteadily into the kitchen and down the basement steps.

"*Nooo!*" she wailed miserably. "*Nooo! They* are down there. I won't go! *Nooo!*"

I heard a howling as I left my sister to fend for herself.

nineteen

Lucky for us, it was not a powerful tornado that swept down our street that day. It skipped around, hitting one house and missing another, almost like it was playing tag with us. I huddled in the basement in a daze. After the storm passed, I hurried upstairs and found Summer curled up in her bed with the covers over her head. She was not hurt.

Except for the swing set, which had been flung into the street, there was no damage to our place. Some of the houses near us had broken windows, and shingles and siding ripped off. Yard furniture was all over the place. But it could have been a whole lot worse, and we learned later that it was pretty bad in other parts of the city.

Henry came over to check on us about ten minutes after I came up from the basement. When I answered the door, he took one look at me and said, "Come on, girl, you're hurt. Let's git you to a doctor."

He took it for granted that I had been injured by the

storm. We couldn't get Summer out from under the covers, so we finally had to leave her there alone. I worried about her the whole time I was in the emergency room getting three stitches in my head. But when Henry took me back home, Summer was still in bed, where she stayed for the rest of the day and night.

Neither of us ever mentioned what she had done to me. But I told Poppy, and I watched his weathered face, strained from fear and worry, crumble into pieces.

"She's plum outa hand, Lyric," he said. "I don't see how we can hold on to her."

And I reckon we both recognized that it was time.

On a lovely day toward the end of August, me and Poppy dressed ourselves and Summer in our finest clothes, and keeping her firmly between us, we walked silently out to the bus stop.

When Poppy paused to tie his shoe, I felt Summer tugging at my sleeve and saying my name, "Lyric."

I turned to her. "Yeah? What is it, Summer?"

"Lyric, I'll be good," she whispered pitifully, and pleaded with her eyes. "I promise."

I looked into that anguished face, and it like to broke my heart. So she knew where we were going, I thought.

I put my arm around her. "Oh, Summer, you *are* good, you are as good as you *can* be!"

And it was the truth. She could no more control her behavior than she could fly away from the wolves. But the monster disease was in charge now, slowly but surely turning my once gentle, bright-eyed sister into a dark angry stranger.

We placed Summer between us on the long back seat of the bus to Pontiac, so that we could both hold on to her, but she was still as we drove through the green countryside.

It's funny how I remember little details of that trip. For instance, I remember the fragrance of some sweet wild bloom on a breeze from an open window. I knew I would never forget that aroma, and if I should ever smell it again, it would bring this moment back to me.

"Smell that?" I whispered to Summer.

Her eyes darted to my face, then Poppy's, but she didn't say anything.

I remember that the bus driver was whistling "Poor People of Paris." It was a real popular song that year. I had heard Poppy whistling it himself quite a lot, but right then his face was old and the saddest I had ever seen it. He did not feel like whistling.

I remember a young man and woman in front of us were sleeping with their heads together. Both snoring. I thought of what Summer had said that time about planning your tomorrows in your sleep. I figured those two were making their plans together and I couldn't help wondering if they ever dreamed the same dream.

I also remember arriving at the *place*, where a large friendly sign read *Welcome to Pontiac State Hospital*, like people might be entering these grounds to attend a party or something. I glanced at Summer to see if she had seen it. But she was leaning sideways and staring intently out the window up at the sky. I wondered what she saw up there.

We entered a huge red brick building where there was a man in the hallway barking like a dog. We steered Summer clear of him. There was also a woman pacing and jabbering nonsense words, just the way Summer was apt to do.

In a front office we were greeted by a young, pretty dark-haired nurse who Summer thought for sure was Jennifer Jones.

"I loved you in *The Song of Bernadette*," she gushed to the nurse, suddenly becoming very friendly. It was almost like she had found something solid to hang on to in deep water. "I'm going to be an actress, too. You will help me, won't you?"

"Yes," the nurse said. "I will."

"I can sing, too," Summer went on happily.

While Poppy signed some papers, I remember thinking how pleasant it would be for Summer to have someone she believed was Jennifer Jones to look after her.

I don't think Summer wanted to know where she was or even *who* she was. We said goodbye, and she didn't watch us walk away from her. She was busy talking to Jennifer Jones.

"I usta be big. Then my shadow left me. I am the Incredible Shrinking Man. The President is experimenting with a cure."

The nurse was smiling at her, and I could tell she was kind. We heard someone screaming far off down a dark corridor as we left, and me and Poppy looked at each other with terror and torment in our eyes.

So we took her there and left her with strangers 'cause we didn't know what else to do. And we went back home and started a strange new life, a life without Summer in it.

It was something of a relief not to have to worry about what to do with her all the time when we had to go here and we had to go there.

We didn't have to think about it anymore.

We could just go with an easy mind.

So we were free.

Still, we found it awful hard and painful to fill up that great big old gaping hole in our lives where Summer had been.

And sometimes in my sleep I could hear her whispering, "I'll be good, Lyric, I promise."

Oh, Summer, Summer, I had to let go!

A few days later when we arrived at the hospital for our first visit, Summer was curled up in a ball in her bed, the same way she had been that first day after coming home from Central High School. She wouldn't talk or even peek out at us. Just laid there she did, curled tight into herself.

Jennifer Jones told us Summer had had a bad reaction to one of her treatments. So we asked what did they do to her.

"ECT—it's electric shock therapy," Jennifer Jones answered matter-of-factly, like she was talking about aspirin or cough syrup. "It's a common treatment for schizophrenia, and usually very effective. But for some reason Summer reacted negatively."

Me and Poppy looked at each other in alarm.

"Electric shock?" Poppy said. "What do you mean?"

"It means we use electricity to disrupt the brain patterns."

"You shocked her brain?" Poppy cried out with a trembling in his voice.

"Well, yes, in a way . . . but what's wrong, Mr. Compton?"

Poppy had sunk to a chair beside Summer's bed and dropped his head on the bed beside hers. It was the only time I ever saw him cry.

Dr. Solomon seemed real smart and kind. We told him how scared of electricity Summer had always been, and he said they would not shock her anymore. He added that it didn't help her anyways.

By our next visit she had come out of her deep withdrawal, but we saw the real Summer only in little bits and pieces after that. And it was painfully clear to me that she really was disappearing. Even though the doctors and nurses were very good, they couldn't seem to bring our Summer back. I talked to Dr. Solomon again, and asked him if she was going to get better.

"We hope to take her home with us again someday," I said.

"I'll not lie to you, Lyric," Dr. Solomon said seriously. "You won't ever again see that pretty, vivacious teenager who *was* your sister. She is gone. I have never known a schizophrenic to recover completely."

He didn't have to say that. He didn't have to take away all of my hope. At least he could have said, "Hang on." So I didn't like Dr. Solomon after that, 'cause he was the man with the watch on, and he had told me the right time.

twenty

I read once that there is a purpose and a lesson even in bad things. I figured the main thing I had learned from what happened to Summer was to be more compassionate toward people who are different.

Like one day I helped a blind man cross the street, and he said, "God bless you, little girl." He couldn't see that I was all grown up.

Another time I saw a woman fall down, and I helped her back on her feet. I smelled liquor when I got close to her, but I went right on helping her, 'cause I felt compassion.

But surely God wouldn't let my sister go crazy just to teach me that! There had to be more to it. No, I figured there had to be something in this experience for everybody. I reckon Poppy learned a lot too. And the doctors and nurses learned more about mental illness.

And what of Summer herself? With her poor muddled mind like it was, it was real hard to tell if she had learned anything a'tall. But surely on some level she had to be the chief learner of us all, because wasn't she the chief sufferer? I didn't really understand all of it, this theory of everything happening for a purpose, but I had to believe it was true. Else, what was it all for?

On Labor Day the city was planning a street dance on the brick pavement downtown. They were advertising fireworks and carnival stuff. I dressed up pretty. I polished my fingernails with Summer's Precious Pink nail polish, and put on my matching lipstick. Then I went down there with Gladys, Nadine, and Yolanda.

Some boys flirted with us, and one of them asked me for my phone number. I just fluttered my eyelids at him, tossed my brown hair away from my face, and in my best Yankee accent I said, "I know you just wanna break my heart, Cutie Pie."

Gladys and Nadine and Yolanda looked at me with admiring eyes. I could tell they were thinking it was a feisty thing to say.

The wound in my heart hurt then. It was still fresh. Given time, I knew it would heal over, leaving only a thin blue scar. In fact, I had a brief vision of myself bumping into that tender place again in the middle of a dark winter's night somewhere in the misty future.

"Where'd you get that scar, Lyric?" I might ask myself then.

"That scar? Oh, when I was a little girl back in the hills, I had a beautiful sister, but . . ."

In our brightly colored summer dresses, we danced with the boys in the street. Laughing and whirling around and around, we were like fireflies, flitting and glowing in the summer dusk.

MEMORIES
of SUMMER

by Ruth White

A READERS GUIDE

★ *"Summer's swift and certain descent
into mental illness . . . is documented
in Lyric's poignant words."*

—KIRKUS REVIEWS, Starred

Questions for Discussion

1. What is special about the relationship between Lyric and Summer? How does it change during the course of the novel?

2. Lyric dreams of buying lavender dresses and lace curtains for her move to Michigan. What does this tell you about Lyric's character and her life?

3. "Even though the teachers at Zimmerman Junior High didn't know my family tree clear back to its roots in England the way the teachers in Virginia did, they treated me like I was a real person anyways. Some of them even made me feel special." (p. 25) Discuss the role teachers play in Lyric's life and how she feels about them.

4. Lyric learns from reading Mark Twain "that it's better to keep your mouth shut and appear stupid, than to open it and remove any doubt." (p. 47) When does Lyric follow this advice? When were some times *you* should have done the same?

5. Lyric is very poor by our standards, but her life is rich in other areas. What are they? Discuss the things that really matter in your life.

6. Lyric is a teenager with a single parent and a sick sister she has to watch over. Any person would be overwhelmed by such responsibility. How does Lyric cope with this?

7. Lyric dreams wolves are chasing her and Summer. Lyric escapes, but she can't save Summer. She has to let go to save herself. Judging by the dream, how does Lyric feel about the situation with Summer?

8. Mama tells Poppy why she named her first child Summer: "She'll grow up just a'sparklin' with warmth and laughter, and the world will be a brighter place with her in it." (p. 3) Discuss the irony of Summer's name. It can be said that Summer burns so brightly that she burns out. What do you think about this statement?

9. The words from one of the songs Lyric listens to—*Summer turns to winter/And the present disappears* (p. 49)—can be seen as a metaphor for Summer's life. Discuss the meaning of this metaphor. How does it relate to what Summer tells Lyric about her mental illness? What does this indicate about Summer's knowledge of herself?

10. "Summer always did have funny ways about her, but I got so used to them, they seemed normal to me." (p. 7) What are some of the odd things Summer does? Why don't Lyric and Poppy recognize this behavior as mental illness?

11. Read aloud the scene in chapter 16 in which Summer unexpectedly shows up during the tryouts for *The Mikado*. Talk about the wide range of emotions Lyric feels—from anger to sadness to grief to a sense of responsibility.

12. Lyric's family has roots in the Virginia hills that go back many generations. Yet when they are given the chance to move north, away from their home, they jump at it. Why are they so eager to move? Discuss the meaning of home in the book and in your life. How do you feel about the place where you live?

13. Seven months after the family has moved from Glory Bottom, Lyric is hard pressed to remember the faces of her kinfolk and the names of her friends. She muses that her new life has made the past fade away. Is this process inevitable? What are some of the ways people can keep continuity in their lives?

14. "'I'll not lie to you, Lyric,' Dr. Solomon said seriously. 'You won't ever again see that pretty, vivacious teenager who *was* your sister.' He didn't have to take away all of my hope. At least he could have said, 'Hang on.' So I didn't like Dr. Solomon after that, 'cause he was the man with the watch on, and he had told me the right time." (p. 132)

What does Lyric mean by this expression? When has someone told you a truth you weren't prepared to hear? Discuss whether we are better off with a false sense of hope or the truth.

This guide was prepared by Clifford Wohl, educational consultant.

In Her Own Words

A CONVERSATION
with
RUTH WHITE

Beth Agresta

Q. Who are the authors who have most influenced your writing?

A. I would have to say Laura Ingalls Wilder was my first and greatest influence. My mother read all of her books to me as I was growing up. In fact, one of my fondest memories is of the entire family piling into one bed while Mama read to us from the Little House books. Recently, I heard of a family who did the same thing with one of my books, and I was very pleased to hear it. Harper Lee's *To Kill a Mockingbird* would have to be right up there at the top as the book having the most influence on my style. That is probably my most favorite book of all time.

Q. Often, writers have a special need to write a story. What was yours in writing *Memories of Summer*?

A. Yes, this was one of those books that I had a special need to write. It was psychotherapy. My oldest sister, Audrey, was schizophrenic, and she began to show the first signs shortly after our family moved to Flint, Michigan, in 1955. Naturally, it was a terribly difficult time for her, but I didn't realize until many years later how traumatic it was for me as well. Much of *Memories* is true. The title came to me when the book was only a ghost in the back of my mind. But no one can write a readable story about schizophrenia without fictionalizing it. It is too painful.

Q. How difficult was it for you to create a character, develop deep affection for her, and then have to depict her disintegration?

A. How difficult was it? Very difficult, because my real sister, Audrey, was very much like Summer. I don't feel that she was my creation at all. In all of my other books, there is something of myself and of my own experiences as a child. I have written about the sad things, and then given myself moderately happy endings, regardless of what the reality was. There is tremendous satisfaction in rewriting history in that way. But no matter how much I wanted to give Summer a happy ending, it simply was not there for her. It could not be there even in fiction.

Q. The relationship of the sisters Lyric and Summer is one of the sweetest aspects of the novel. Is this relationship built on personal experience?

A. Not in reality. Audrey was five years older than I. But as I was writing and looking back on that time, I saw everything through older and wiser eyes, and I felt a compassion for my sister that made me want to go back and be there for her. So once again, I rewrote history by giving Summer a warm and loving relationship with her younger sister.

Q. In teen fiction, teachers are often depicted as being unsympathetic. In *Memories of Summer*, the teachers are portrayed as kind and understanding, and they play pivotal roles in saving Lyric from the trauma she encounters. Why are teachers so important to you?

A. Because I feel my teachers did save me in reality. Many of them played important roles in helping me to mature, to find my place in the world, and to look to the future with hope.

There really was a Mr. German, who was my music teacher that year, and a very special person. There really was a Mrs. Gaspar, but I did not meet her until 1986. In that year, I met a wonderful elderly lady in Virginia Beach, who I learned had been teaching music in the Flint public school system in 1955, but not at Zimmerman, where I attended. I wanted to include her in the book anyway.

Today I am a firm believer that every person who comes into our lives has something to teach us and something to learn from us. So we are all teachers.

Q. Music comes up a lot in the novel. Can you talk about the importance of music in the lives of your characters?

A. Music is a source of great joy and a creative outlet for many of my characters, as it has always been for me. Music was very important to me as I was growing up, and given the opportunity, I believe I would have found a career in that field. But there was no money for lessons, nor was music given serious consideration in our home. Writing, on the other hand, my other major interest, was also a creative and emotional outlet, and didn't cost anything.

Q. What is your favorite scene in the novel and why?

A. I think my favorite scene is the trip to Flint and the first week there. Why? Mainly because it was Summer and Lyric's happiest time together.

The most consistent compliment I receive on my work is the statement "Your books seem so real!" They seem real because they *are* real in many ways. As I wrote this scene, I was remembering the real trip to Flint in September of 1955, on a Greyhound bus. I tried to include in the story every memory I had of that first week to give my story its reality. To me that whole part of the story is a step back into the past.

Q. This novel is rich in details—large and small—about life in Appalachia and Michigan during the 1950s. What kind of research did you do?

A. No research whatsoever. I relied solely on my memory. I keep a mental filing cabinet of those years in the hills of Virginia, and also of the move to Flint. Sometimes I ask my sisters for their input, but for the most part, the memories are all mine.

Q. The bond between Lyric and her roots in Appalachia begins to break down as the story unfolds. Can you tell if Lyric will ever be able to "go home again"?

A. If Lyric stays in Flint, she will never be able to go home again. She is now a part of a bigger world, which at that time had more to offer than Glory Bottom did. She will always remember her home in the hills, but her memories will grow dim with time as she becomes more and more involved in her new life. If she ever goes back to visit her friends and relatives there, she will not be comfortable.

On the other hand, in reality, I did "go home again." I never got over my homesickness, but I stayed with my family in Flint for a year. At the end of that year I returned to my roots, moved in with an aunt and uncle, and lived there throughout high school. My novel *Weeping Willow* is based on those years.

After high school I left, but even today, I return about once a year to see old friends. It is a special place.

Q. If *Memories of Summer* were set as a contemporary novel, how different would it be?

A. I don't think it would make a good contemporary novel. The conflict would not be the same. The treatment of mental illness has vastly improved, and people are more open-minded about it.

American Academy of Child & Adolescent Psychiatry

Facts for families about schizophrenia as well as other mental disorders affecting children and adolescents.

www.aacap.org/publications/factsfam/schizo.htm

National Institute of Mental Health

Information on the causes of and treatments for schizophrenia.

www.nimh.nih.gov/publicat/schizoph.htm

My Appalachia

Poetry, photographs, and descriptions of Appalachia, as well as a list of regional authors.

www.users.kih.net/~bunderwood

CVA—Center for Virtual Appalachia

A portal to information about Appalachia's people, culture, and environment.

http://cva.morehead-st.edu

Rabble Starkey
LOIS LOWRY
0-440-40056-2
This beautifully written novel tells the story of
twelve-year-old Rabble, who lives in a small Appalachian
town with her mother.

A Summer to Die
LOIS LOWRY
0-440-21917-5
Sibling rivalry is nothing new for Meg and her older
sister, Molly, but one summer will change everything
between them.

Bud, Not Buddy
CHRISTOPHER PAUL CURTIS
0-440-41328-1
In this Newbery Award Winner, Bud's search for
his father brings adventure during a trip through
Depression-era Michigan.

Kissing Doorknobs
TERRY SPENCER HESSER
0-440-41314-1
An inspiring, humorous novel about one girl's
experience with obsessive-compulsive disorder.

Kit's Wilderness
DAVID ALMOND
0-440-41605-1

Kit Watson and John Askew look for the childhood ghosts of
their long-gone ancestors in the mines of Stoneygate.

Skellig
DAVID ALMOND
0-440-22908-1

Michael feels helpless because of his baby sister's
illness, until he meets a creature called Skellig.

Heaven Eyes
DAVID ALMOND
0-440-22910-3

Erin Law and her friends in the orphanage are labeled
Damaged Children. They run away one night, traveling
downriver on a raft. What they find on their journey is
stranger than you can imagine.
Available October 2002

Becoming Mary Mehan—Two Novels
JENNIFER ARMSTRONG
0-440-22961-8

Set against the events of the American Civil War,
The Dreams of Mairhe Mehan depicts an Irish immigrant girl
and her family who are struggling to find their place in the
war-torn country. *Mary Mehan Awake* takes up Mary's story
after the war, when she must begin a journey of renewal.

Forgotten Fire
ADAM BAGDASARIAN
0-440-22917-0

In 1915, Vahan Kenderian is living a life of privilege when his world is shattered by the Turkish-Armenian War.

Ghost Boy
IAIN LAWRENCE
0-440-41668-X

Fourteen-year-old Harold Kline is an albino—an outcast. When the circus comes to town, Harold runs off to join it in hopes of discovering who he is and what he wants in life. Is he a circus freak or just a normal guy?

Gathering Blue
LOIS LOWRY
0-440-22949-9

Lamed and suddenly orphaned, Kira is mysteriously removed to live in the palatial Council Edifice, where she is expected to use her gifts as a weaver to do the bidding of the all-powerful Guardians.
Available September 2002

The Giver
LOIS LOWRY
0-440-23768-8

Jonas's world is perfect. Everything is under control. There is no war or fear or pain. There are no choices, until Jonas is given an opportunity that will change his world forever.
Available September 2002

Both Sides Now
RUTH PENNEBAKER
0-440-22933-2

A compelling look at breast cancer through the eyes of a mother and daughter. Liza must learn a few life lessons from her mother, Rebecca, about the power of family.
Available July 2002

Her Father's Daughter
MOLLIE POUPENEY

0-440-22879-4

As she matures from a feisty tomboy of seven to a
spirited young woman of fourteen, Maggie discovers
that the only constant in her life of endless new
homes and new faces is her ever-emerging
sense of herself.

The Baboon King
ANTON QUINTANA

0-440-22907-3

Neither Morengáru's father's Masai tribe nor his
mother's Kikuyu tribe accepts him. Banished from
both tribes, Morengáru encounters a baboon troop
and faces a fight with the simian king.

Holes
LOUIS SACHAR

0-440-22859-X

Stanley has been unjustly sent to a boys' detention
center, Camp Green Lake. But there's more than
character improvement going on at the camp—
the warden is looking for something.

Memories of Summer
RUTH WHITE

0-440-22921-9

In 1955, thirteen-year-old Lyric describes her older
sister Summer's descent into mental illness, telling
Summer's story with humor, courage, and love.